D0575859

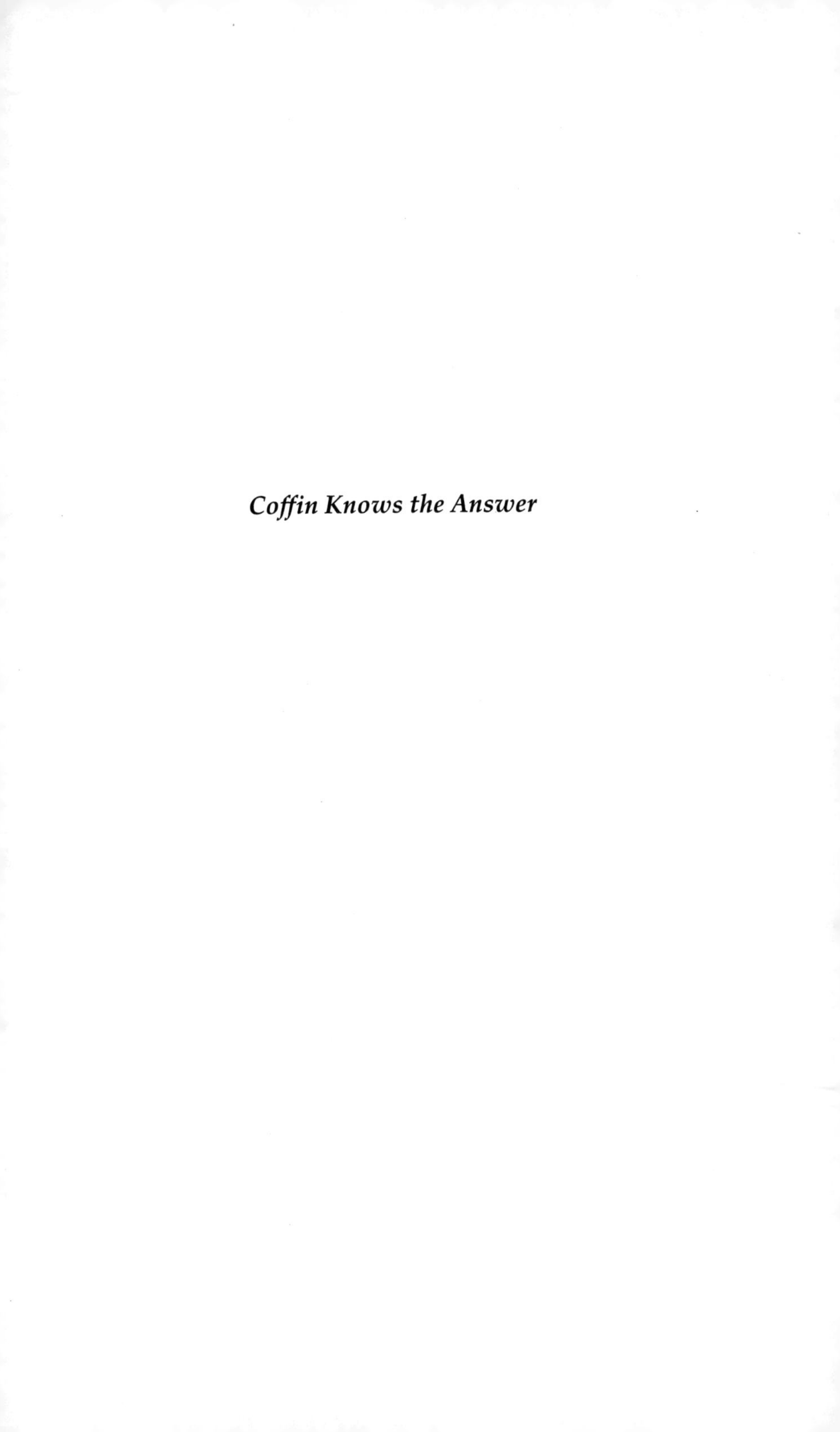

Coffin Knows the Answer

Coffin Knows the Answer

GWENDOLINE BUTLER

First published in Great Britain in 2002 by
Allison & Busby Limited
Suite 111, Bon Marche Centre
241-251 Ferndale Road
Brixton, London SW9 8BJ
http://www.allisonandbusby.ltd.uk

Copyright © 2002 by GWENDOLINE BUTLER

The right of Gwendoline Butler to be identified as
author of this work has been asserted by her in
accordance with the Copyright, Designs and
Patents Act, 1988

This book is sold subject to the condition that it shall not,
by way of trade or otherwise, be lent, resold, hired out or
otherwise circulated without the publisher's prior
written consent in any form of binding or cover other than
that in which it is published and without a similar condition
including this condition being imposed upon the subsequent
purchaser.

A catalogue record for this book is available from the British Library

ISBN 0 7490 0542 4

Printed and bound in Spain by
Liberdúplex, s. l. Barcelona

GWENDOLINE BUTLER was born in Blackheath, London. A winner of the CWA Silver Dagger Award, she has written over fifty books.

Chapter 1

'What would you call the worst crime in the world? '

Coffin looked towards DCI Phoebe Astley who was studying some notes from a file on his desk. They dealt with a fraud case she had just completed.

They were old friends, Phoebe enjoyed working with him. Coffin was the most stable element in her life which sometimes felt more like a two-way escalator, down and up shifting with speed.

'Oh, I don't know,' said Phoebe absently. 'Kicking your old grandmother down the stairs. Torching her cat. Gassing a million...' She stopped because the Chief Commander had pushed a photograph in front of her.

'Oh my God.'

'Yes. Six months old.' Under his breath, he muttered something she did not catch. He pushed another photograph towards her. 'He was three years and a bit.'

Phoebe looked sick. In her time as a police officer she had seen plenty of horrors, but children, babies, still hit her hardest. Yes, this was the worst of crimes. One for which she would be willing to kill the perp or perps. That was the other horror, it was a group thing. They needed an audience for their crime.

Coffin flipped another set of pictures towards her. She looked at the photographs on the Chief Commander's desk. The perps needed a record as well, pictures to look at in the bedroom or bathroom at home.

Phoebe looked across to Coffin, now Sir John Coffin, Chief Commander of Police in the Second City of London. He looked tired. She felt tired herself, engaged as she had been in a long investigation now ended with a satisfactory result. Three people committed for trial for fraud and murder. Women too. Women were getting more violent, no doubt about it.

She felt violent herself as she studied the photographs of abused and violated infants.

Then Coffin looked at her and smiled. At once she felt less weary.

'It's good work you've done on the Wantage fraud case, Phoebe,' he said. 'But I may be asking you to take on this paedophile business... '

'Who else is working on it?'

'Joe Jones and Mercy Adams, but Joe has just been diagnosed with leukaemia and I think that is going to take all his energies for a bit. And apparently Mercy is worried she might be pregnant.'

'Oh.' Phoebe was disconcerted. Joe was a good worker, sometimes tricky to handle, but clever. She had heard that he had come close to a breakdown. She didn't know exactly what that meant but he had sounded pretty rocky. As for Mercy, well she was a widow or divorced so who was the father? (If she *was* pregnant... she had had worries before). Was it that young doctor she was so keen on?

'The word is he is going to be all right,' Coffin continued, 'but he needs help.'

What sort of help, Phoebe wondered. 'How will it be if I go to see him? Has anyone else been?'

'Mercy went, of course, she says that his wife has set up a strong protective shield.'

A strong lady, tall and muscular, as Phoebe remembered her, and not much liked by Mercy who was small-boned and pretty. Josephine Jones was handsome but not pretty. She worked in the local hospital, so was well placed to watch over her husband.

Would Mercy mind Phoebe taking over? The answer was certainly yes, but she would have to put up with it. You did not argue with John Coffin in certain moods. Not unless you were his wife, Stella.

'It's all right,' said Coffin, as if he had guessed what she was thinking 'Mercy will co-operate, I've had a word with her, she wants this business cleared up as much as I do.' He put his hands together, staring at them, assessing the fact that two fingernails were broken. 'She's known for some time that Joe was not working at speed.'

'If you think I can do it.' So now she knew why she had been called into his office, given a cup of coffee and left to think about life while he studied the file of papers and photographs. She could see envelopes and handwritten letters inside.

'Of course you can. You will, you must.'

Thanks for the vote of confidence, she thought. If that was what it was. Am I about to be pushed into something I cannot control?

Coffin read her expression. 'No, nothing like that. I wouldn't drop you into anything.'

John Coffin and Phoebe Astley had known each other for a long time, way back to the days when Phoebe worked in Birmingham before being recruited to the Second City with advanced promotion. She had come because she wanted the promotion and liked the Chief Commander. Their relationship went back to the time which Phoebe called The Days Before Stella. Not quite true because Stella went back a long way in the Chief Commander's life, even if they had been apart for a considerable time. He loved her, though. No doubt about it. Phoebe, not without her own experiences of the tender passions, did not begrudge the Chief Commander what he had found in Stella.

A few of the team that Coffin had carefully gathered around him in the beginning to police the Second City had won promotion and moved. Archie Young was one, and now commanded his own Police Force. Paul Masters, a much younger man, remained still close to the Chief Commander, and then there was Phoebe herself.

'Those first photographs I showed you were not taken by the police team. Not part of this investigation.'

Phoebe nodded.

'No, they came in the post in a plain envelope to the CID office. You could say they started the inquiry. Others followed.'

'Someone must have wanted you to start looking.'

Coffin was silent.

'The second set of photographs I showed you did not come to CID. They came straight to my home.'

'To you there?' Phoebe was questioning. 'I guess they wanted to be sure you got them.'

'Oh no ... they were addressed to Stella. And before you say that was a compliment, it was not.' He tossed more of the photographs towards Phoebe. 'They were not well meant, Stella was meant to feel pain...This is a Stalker, with a paedophile slant.'

His voice set the word Stalker in capital letters.

'Do you think that this stalker is the paedophile?' Phoebe pressed.

'There is a difference in style between these letters and the Stalker,' admitted Coffin.'I sense this but I am not sure if Mercy does'. He added gloomily, 'Two criminals then and not just one'

Phoebe Astley took up the photographs. 'But Stella...' she said incredulously. 'Why Stella, everyone loves Stella?'

Coffin shook his head. 'I'd like to think so but apparently not. May be nothing personal, may be a way of getting at me.'

'Who else is on it besides Joe and Mercy?'

'All there in the file...Ellen Gower is one. You know her.'

Phoebe nodded. Yes, and she liked Ellen, they had worked together before.

Phoebe had been going to take a few days' leave, get her hair done and visit her mother, but she was not going to refuse to take on the job, you did not say No to the Chief Commander who, for all his politeness and quite genuine kindness of heart, was tough.

Another factor: she had been Chief Inspector for a few years and she was looking for promotion.

Not much time to consider, it had to be Yes or No, and it wasn't going to be No. She was conscious of the inquisitive presence of Paul Masters in the other office. She had sometimes had the wry suspicion that he had some sort of listening device because he always seemed to know everything. But probably it was just that he had the Chief Commander's diary and put two and two together.

'Right,' she said.

'Take a few days off to make yourself familiar with the stuff Joe and Mercy have got.'

So she could get her hair done after all. Perhaps he'd looked at it too and thought it needed help. Having a wife like Stella Pinero would certainly give you skill in assessing a woman's grooming. Without thinking, she ran her hand over her hair.

'I might just have a word with Mercy first.' Tactful thing to do, it was possible that Mercy did not mind Phoebe's entrance into the case, but more than likely she would. 'Ask about Joe.'

'She knows you're coming,' said the Chief Commander.

'Yes, sure.' She knew, and he knew, that there would certainly be bits of information, speculation and informed guesses that had not got through to the written record in the files and that she would have to tease out of Mercy like a knot in the hair (there it was, hair again!) just as Mercy allowed. Some interesting thoughts were now in hospital with Joe. That was the worst of coming into a team late.

'Does Mercy know about these photographs sent to your wife?'

'No,' said Coffin sharply. 'You're the first. Stella doesn't know herself, and I'm trusting that I will not have to tell her. Not until she gets back. She's away for the next week filming a TV play in Scotland.'

He stood up to look out of the window. Distantly, he could see the belt of tall trees which hid the bit of unused land where Stella was about to build a tiny new theatre for students. (She would also rent it out, thus raising money). From his office he could see the roof of the theatre where Stella worked. She had created that theatre in the old church of St Luke's - he thought of it as Stella's theatre. They had made their home in the old tower of the church. An eccentric and expensive home but now very attractive and much loved by both Stella and Coffin. Their own too, not a police house, where they lived with the cat and the dog. The dog was with him now, lying on his feet, while the cat was probably out hunting. There was a tiny, disused old cemetery, long since transformed, across the road from St Luke's Tower where mice, squirrels and other wild animals were the cat's prey. A new building was going up next to the theatre complex, it was going to be rehearsal rooms because Stella was developing activities. So far only the foundations were being opened up, he could see the mud and the stones. He guessed the cat would enjoy excavating down there too.

As he thought about the cat, so mild and gentle at home, hunter and killer outside, he remembered his other worry.

It looked as though they had a serial killer in the Second City. Once again he considered the possibility that there was more than one nasty criminal on his territory.

He turned to Phoebe and said 'She's already miserable about the two dead girls. She knew one of them: Amy Buckly, she was the one found by the canal...The other girl, Mary Rice was found near the railway station.'

Raped and strangled.

'I've heard that a third girl has been found dead.' Superintendent Miller and Inspector Winnie Ardet were running the case. Winnie was a friend, Jack Miller was not. But that did not matter, it was sometimes better not to be a friend in this job. Coffin was remembering uneasily a promise he had once made Jack Miller, for reasons he could not now remember, something to the effect that if Jack was ever in any trouble, he could count on Coffin.

Winnie Ardet had been working with a colleague on another nasty crime. Same method and killing, the same sexual assault.

Coffin nodded. 'No doubt about it. We've got a serial killer in the Second City.'

'Not the first.'

'No, there was a local who went berserk and did a run of killings not long after I took over, but I don't think he was a true serial killer, he killed friends and relations. He was soon caught. He'd almost run out of likely victims.'

Phoebe was never quite sure whether to laugh or not at one of Coffin's wry jokes. This time she decided not to.

'Winnie was talking to me about it earlier. She thinks this one is coming on strong.'

'Winnie may be right,' he said dourly.

No jokes today, Phoebe said to herself. The paedophile and the serial killer are really getting to him and who can blame him?

And he is missing Stella. Phoebe had known the Chief Commander long enough to notice undertones in his voice when they were there. He could probably do the same for her. Almost certainly he knew that she didn't fancy the paedophile ring investigation, and he also knew that for this very reason she would put her back into it.

'I'll get along to talk to Mercy and go through the files and whatever she's got on the computer.'

And since the Chief Commander had suggested she take a little time off, she would get her hair cut and washed. However, she knew from experience that his idea of time off was a cup of coffee in the canteen and then back to the job. So she would have to go canny.

The dog, old Gus, shifted position under the Chief Commander's desk, then came out looking sleepy. Gus was an elderly pekinese, not in very good health (heart pills after a heart transplant, something for his kidneys and the odd painkiller for his rheumatism), but still enjoying life. He had survived the much-loved cat, enjoying a period of autonomy and peace before the arrival of a new cat. Because the new creature had large, appealing eyes, Stella had decided it was a female, to be named something soft and gentle like Angel or Honey. When taken to the vet for her immunisation, worming and anti-flea injections, however, the vet had gently pointed out that Angel was in fact a well-endowed male. An emasculating snip or two had been performed so that Angel had returned home as a tom. He was now a large cat who may have lost some of his sexual drive but none of his aggression or sharpness.

'When's Stella getting back?' Phoebe enquired.

'Another week if I'm lucky, might go on a bit longer.' He smiled. 'I hope sooner rather than later. I'm looking after Gus and the cat: I need help.'

'I'd be glad to do anything I could, sir.'

'I might take you up on that.'

The small clock on his desk chimed. The clock had been Stella's Christmas gift, or one of them as she was prodigal with presents, so that although Coffin hated the idea of a clock with a bell, he went on using it. He was beginning to find it useful to remind him of what he might be tempted to forget or pretend he had forgotten, a device he was not above using. In his office outside he had two secretaries both too tactful to remind him of appointments too obviously. He had them well trained.

Gus, the white peke, stood still as if he knew what the bell meant.

'Go back,' said Coffin. 'Not time for your walk yet.'

'I'll take him, if you like. He knows me.'

Gus gave a small movement of his tail. Yes, it said, he knew her. He stood up hopefully. Phoebe stood up too.

'I'll give you his lead. Don't let him off however much he

asks because he runs off. Last time he got in a laundry van and had to be brought back from Greenwich.'

Gus was hooked up and ready to go when the telephone rang. 'Hang on a moment, Phoebe.'

Gus and Phoebe stood by the door, both listening while pretending not to. Not much good being a detective, Phoebe had always thought, if you can't listen to other people's conversations when you want to.

'Yes, Paul. Put him through. Miller? Yes, I did say that I wanted to know at once of any thing vital...' He listened, his face serious and intent. 'This is the body that just turned up. On Pilling Common?'

Pilling Common sounded romantic and rustic, as it may have been before being swallowed up by factories and docks. Even the docks were disused now and the factories empty. The whole district was being redeveloped into flats and offices, which would all be expensive and smart. A small remnant of what had once been open space deserving of the name of a piece of common ground was still there as a municipal park.

'Right, Miller, thank you for telling me. Keep me in touch.' He looked at Phoebe and Gus, hardly seeing them.

'Something happened?' asked Phoebe.

'I wanted to be kept informed. That was Superintendant Jack Miller doing just that.'

Coffin liked to be involved in the serious cases, more so than perhaps he should have done, but you couldn't kill the detective in him. Most of the CID officers accepted this, gratefully in some cases, less so in other. Jack Miller was one of the less grateful.

'I won't interfere,' said Coffin, thoughtfully and aloud.

Phoebe knew he would, and that they'd be grateful if he did. So, he might miss a committee or two in London that he was meant to be at, but the Second City would be the better for it.

'The new girl,' he said. 'The new victim, she was only a girl, strangled and raped, no semen, must have used a condom, every detail just the same. But a bit extra this time: she was cut open... '

'Nasty.' Phoebe could feel Gus settle himself across her feet. It was his way of telling her to get a move on.

'The Ripper was like that... got more and more to enjoy the sensation of cutting into flesh.'

'I suppose it's pleasure,' Phoebe said doubtfully.

'Not what you and I would call pleasure... but an excitement, a glow ... the knife was sharp enough to cut through the flesh and muscle but blunt enough to drag at it.'

'Is that what Jack Miller said?' Sounded too vivid for him.

Coffin gave her a half smile. 'He just gave me the idea.' He bent down to pat Gus. 'We've got to get him.'

'Before he gets really nasty?'

Another smile. 'Bloody old world, isn't it? All young women... just out walking. One of them even had her dog with her.'

He looked down at his own small dog, asleep on his feet.

'How's Stella?' asked Phoebe. She knew that Lady Pinero had been very busy with the scholarship auditions she had been holding through which the chosen candidate would get offered training as well as a part.

'One lucky lad is chosen.'

'And her new theatre?'

'Well, the auditioning and so on has brought her the publicity she hoped for, and now she has to face the actual building work.' He smiled affectionately.

'And that's on the way?'

'Starts very soon.'

The phone rang, and this time it was what Phoebe knew to be his private line. 'Stella? Lovely to hear your voice. How are you? Oh good. How is the work going?' He smiled, so work was going well. 'A box... Do you want me to collect it?...Yes sure, of course. I'll take the dog and walk round there. What do you want me to do with it... Right.'

He hung up and turned to Phoebe. 'She's had a message to say that a parcel is waiting for her in St Luke's Tower. She thinks it's some new makeup she ordered... Doesn't want it sitting in the sun.'

'Might get nicked' Phoebe said. 'Can't I collect it for you and bring it back here with Gus?

Coffin considered.

'I'd like the walk with the dog... while I think over this paedophile case you want me into.'

'Well in,' said Coffin, making it almost a command. 'That's what it needs, Joe and Mercy have been floating the surface a bit.'

'I suppose Joe wasn't fit. And Mercy had a row with that doctor she's been seeing.'

'Make them more determined to get the perpetrators. Keener.'

'But frightened too.'

Coffin was silent. Then he said: 'No names have been mentioned in the press or on TV. Joe and Mercy have not been mentioned.'

'No,' said Phoebe.

More silence. Coffin took a deep breath. 'I won't pretend I don't know what you are getting at. Or that I have not considered it.'

Phoebe waited.

'The paedophile group may contain one or more people I know.'

'And who work with... us.'

'Possibly a member or members of the Second City Force.' said Coffin. 'And Joe and Mercy will have sensed this. That's about it, isn't it?'

Phoebe nodded. 'Yes.'

'Well, I agree with you. And it's one of the reasons I have asked you to take charge. How does that make you feel?'

Phoebe took a deep breath. 'That I want to get on with it,

sir.' She looked down at the dog, 'Come on, Gus, we'll take that walk.'

On the stairs in the theatre she passed a tall, thin youth who was, although she did not know it, Andrew Eliot, the lad who had won Stella's prize audition and who would be working in Spinnerwick. He bowed and smiled at Phoebe, who smiled back. She liked good looking youths. Andrew was doing secretarial work at the police station to earn money for a nose job, to make him even more good looking for his acting career.

As she set out with Gus, trotting cheerfully in front as if ready to walk miles (although she knew from past experience, he would soon be looking up and saying he couldn't walk another step and now could she carry him), her thoughts were not focused on the dog.

She wondered how Mercy would take her arrival in charge. Mercy, polite and friendly as she was, had the reputation of protecting her own territory.

And then there was the matter of her love affair. Since her divorce Mercy could be tricky. Phoebe had never been quite sure if Mercy was divorced or widowed. Both was her secret opinion: divorced then remarried and widowed. She certainly had a taste for men.

Joe had surely declared his position by falling ill. All right, he didn't invent it, who would, but she knew Joe well enough to guess that in the normal way he would have carried on working if at all possible.

Phoebe went up to her small office on the third floor. Would she still be working from there when she got into the paedophiles? Probably not. A bigger office would be necessary, but she would be back here, it was the nearest place to her working home since she had left Birmingham.

She rang Mercy, with Gus sitting on her feet, looking hurt. Where was that walk? 'Mercy?'

'Oh hello. So you're taking over?' Her voice was brisk and Phoebe had known it friendlier.

'Working *with* you,' said Phoebe, 'that's more the way of it. I didn't get a lot of choice, you don't with the Chief Commander when he's made a decision.'

Mercy knew it. 'It's not a nice piece of cake, you know.'

'Then we needn't eat it like that, need we?'

Mercy laughed and relaxed. 'No, sure. Well, there you are, we do it together.'

'How's Joe?' Phoebe asked.

'Not too bad. Turns out he hasn't got leukaemia, the symptoms looked right but when they did some tests, it wasn't. But he's got to rest.' She added, a shade wistfully: 'He's out of hospital. Home, being cherished.' At least, she thought that was what it was.

Taking a month or so off, thought Phoebe, she couldn't blame him. 'How are you feeling?'

Mercy did not pretend not to understand. 'I expect to keep well. I've sent my son to Fife to stay with family. I think with two brothers who are into judo, not to mention two guard dogs, he will be safe enough.'

'Right.' Phoebe looked down at Gus. And I haven't even got a cat or dog to worry about. Another reason why I got chosen. Perhaps she could get a cat. Or later on, even have a baby. People did, you weren't obliged to have a father, although it was probably nicer, just a little bit of semen. But she could no doubt manage the father if she gave her mind to it. Jokey speculation like that always cheered her up.

'What sort of mood is the Lord High Executioner in? Approachable?' Mercy wanted to know.

'He's always approachable, isn't he?'

'Well, yes,' said Mercy.'

'Sometimes more so. Stella's away, he can be edgy. He's jealous, you see.'

'No!'

'Of course, she's an attractive woman, and it's her job to let people see it. I'm jealous myself sometimes. '

'I never know whether to believe you or not.'

Phoebe laughed.

'Anyway, I want to see him, need to see him, and I hope he will listen to me.'

'Try him and see, 'Phoebe advised.

'Yeah, might do that.'

'I'll be back.' said Phoebe. 'And we'll mop up this paedophile outfit, I'm determined. May be only a small group. Even a one man band, feels to me like that.' And then she was determined she would be transferred to the Stalker investigation.

Phoebe said goodbye to Mercy and then she and Gus trotted off together; Phoebe feeling more cheerful and Gus more determined to get his walk.

On the way, she saw Mercy, also on her way somewhere... 'Hi.'

'As we're soon going to be working together,' Mercy said, 'we'll have to get used to meeting.' She sounded only half pleased at the prospect. 'There's a room for you to work in been found.'

'What's in it?'

'It hasn't been opened yet. Waiting for you, I think...Joke. This is a bloody difficult case.'

Mercy did not know for sure as yet who was going to be in charge now Joe was off. She wanted the job, but Phoebe outranked her. And in fact she had a strong feeling that she was going to be on the outskirts of this case. One of those CID officers who is occasionally seen but seldom heard. A disappearing act which somehow wins promotion. If Phoebe sought to be transferred to the Stalker outfit, then no doubt she would be, Mercy thought.

Anyway, a call on the Chief Commander might settle her mind.

Even as tolerant and polite a Chief Commander as John Coffin (who well remembered his own humbler days) could not be seen without a preliminary talk with Paul Masters who 'kept the book' as he liked to describe it.

He had a desk in one corner of the big room with two acolytes of either sex (one no longer called them secretaries) at their computers and various other electronic aids on longish tables.

Paul had run in the London Marathon once, he and Mercy had trained together and Mercy had got through while he had had to drop out. An experience like that gives you respect for the other person. Liking too in this case, because Mercy had never once made a joke of him. Never even mentioned it, so most of his colleagues, who would certainly have referred more than once to Drop Out Paul, never knew of it.

Paul showed Mercy in, asked Coffin if they would like coffee, and then brought it in. He then tactfully retired. It was up to Mercy now.

Coffin, who knew the value of silence, waited for her to speak.

'Stench.'

The word shattered the silence.

'It smells, you must think so yourself, sir.'

'Certainly it presents some unusual features,' Coffin said cautiously, waiting to hear what she had to say. Did she know about the photographs sent to Stella?

'It seems aimed at us, not personally, but sent on purpose.' So she didn't know about what had come to Stella.

For that matter, Stella herself did not know. Not yet. May be she would never have to.

'That's what had Joe puzzled. I don't say it made him ill, of course it didn't, but by God, it helped. ' And maybe he wasn't as ill as he acted; he just wanted out.

'In these cases we have to seek out evidence of paedophilia. You know we do: it's a secret activity and they want it kept secret.' Mercy continued.

'Except among themselves,' said Coffin

'It's almost a proxy activity, the passing round of the photographs is as important as the activity itself.'

'Pleasure enjoyed in remembrance,' said Coffin.

'And we're part of the pleasure: the police team, you even, sir.' she did not see Coffin give an imperceptible flinch, 'and we don't like it. I don't like it , Joe didn't like it. Phoebe won't like it when she gets a whiff of it.'

'Yes,' agreed Coffin.

'As a rule we have to go searching, but now it is coming at us and we don't have to look, it is supplied. By the perpetrators? Not something they usually do. This case is not typical, I can feel it.'

Coffin nodded.

Mercy stood up. 'Thank you for seeing me and letting me talk... I just wanted to let you know how uneasy Joe and I have been. In case anything goes wrong.'

'Do you think it will?'

Mercy nodded. 'Could do. But how and what I can't tell... just a feeling.'

'Feelings count,' said Coffin, speaking from memories of his past.

'I hear that another body has arrived in our area, courtesy of the killer of the other girls?'

Coffin nodded.

'No connection with the paedophiles?'

'Not as far as I know. If you find one, let me know.' He was holding the door for her.

Never forgets he's a gentleman as well as the Boss, thought Mercy. 'At once, sir.'

She deserved a smile from him and got it.

Phoebe and Gus took a leisurely walk through the little old churchyard, now a small park and then turned back to the tower where Coffin and Stella had made their home. Three stone steps led up to the front door. Phoebe had half convinced herself that she would find nothing, but there was a small parcel lying on the grey stone.

It was addressed to Stella.

'Right, Gus, we'll take it to your master.'

The parcel, in thick brown paper, typed address, was square and while not heavy just a trifle more solid than she had expected.

Managing Gus who was keen to get back to Coffin, she dropped the parcel. 'Shook that up a bit,' she said as she picked it up. 'Don't suppose it matters.'

They walked up the stairs to Coffin's office since Gus did not like either the lift or the escalator and passed Paul Masters with a wave.

'What's that you've got there?' Masters asked.

Phoebe shook her head and marched in to the Chief Commander's office.

She handed the parcel over to Coffin who was seated at his desk, then looked at it. 'Something's leaked,' she said. 'I dropped it, what did I do when I dropped it?'

She stared at her hand. 'It's blood.'

Coffin took the packet from her, ripped off the paper, increasingly wet with blood. Inside was a tin that had once held biscuits, the lid had been dislodged when it fell. Perhaps it had never fitted very well, nor the packer cared.

In the box, swimming in its own blood, was a body organ.

'Human,' said Coffin bluntly. Not dog, cat or horse but human, he was sure.

'A ute,' whispered Phoebe, she had done some premed stuff at university which had included anatomy. 'I don't think it's human, though. Wrong size.'

'I know it is a uterus,' said Coffin, half to himself. 'And there is a certain opacity which suggests there is an embryo inside.'

'It's part of the paedophile crimes, I'm sure, damn it. I knew they were building up to even more nastiness.'

Through the blood he could see that the address bore Stella's name.

'Why Stella?'

'I wondered that myself,' said Phoebe.

Stella Pinero, Lady Coffin but she preferred her professional name, was at that moment filming a comedy in Scotland. It was a good part, the best, and the film looked like being a big success. Coffin did not want anything to touch her happiness.

'I've never known Stella more bouyant, or sure that she was doing good work. And she is. I've seen some of the rushes... she could get an award. It matters to her, I couldn't bear to take the shine off that. No, we must just catch the lunatic who's sending these messages. Shouldn't be difficult.'

'You think whoever sent this to Stella knew about her success?'

Coffin shrugged. 'She's had some publicity in the national press recently.' He added: 'I shan't tell Stella.'

'Won't she find out?'

'I won't tell her, and you won't.'

Phoebe knew she would not say anything, but she had a well-founded respect for Stella's ability to winkle things out.

'Perhaps it's aimed more at you than Stella.' She added quietly : 'I expect Mercy will have something cogent to say. I'll get this mess to her, shall I?'

'You're in charge now.'

'Mercy won't like that much.'

'She's out of her depth, and knows it.'

Phoebe was not so sure: Mercy was a clever, hardworking officer. She was also ambitious. 'We've had a talk. And I met her by chance earlier today.'

'Good. Did she say anything?'

'Not much. We'll work together well enough,' Phoebe said.

'I hate the human race sometimes, don't you ,' Coffin said aloud. It wasn't truly a question, but a statement, and a sad one.

Chapter 2

In a car parked near St Luke's House, a man was dealing with a body. He was a strong man but he was struggling.

It is always difficult carrying a woman's body if she does not help. Like putting her arms round your neck, or tucking her legs up neatly. This body was not helping.

Never would help, could not.

'Come on, love,' he said. 'An inflatable doll could be more sexy than you are.'

He had put the car where he and the body could not be overlooked from the theatre area. It was a risk, of course, that he would be seen and he knew that. Cut and run if someone does appear, he told himself. Just go. Or he might call out: Giving the lady a lift home from dinner, had a drop too much. Being English, they would certainly hurry off in embarrassment. But so far he seemed to be managing.

It wasn't easy, though. 'Don't be awkward now... I may have to lop your arm off to get you along.'

Somehow the notion pleased him.

As he moved forward, he was trying to decide where to leave the body. Inside the house or outside in the garden?

He was not entirely a free agent: he thought he could get into the house and take her with him. There were difficulties: actually getting inside he knew he could manage, but then there was the dog. There was a cat but he did not expect trouble there, cats were different, they had their thoughts and their claws, but leave them alone and they would leave you alone.

He found his decision was made. Inside it was. 'Off we go, baby.'

In spite of the owner's efficient security treatment of his house, the man thought he knew how to gain entrance.

He got himself in first, then went back for the body. He did have to deal with the arm, but he twisted it back without too much trouble. He always carried a knife, but a knife would not do here.

'I am not mad,' he told himself. 'Eccentric, I will accept. This is me having an eccentric joke with you, lady.'

A wave of nausea swept through him. This was not the place to be sick, better get the job done. Since he couldn't be pregnant, it was time to get home.

Chapter 3

Coffin went home after speaking to Phoebe, where he fed the dog and the cat. Stella had taken care to provide a variety of tins and packets, all of which the animals were said to like. He spooned the food, a fishy mixture for the cat, meaty for Gus, into the dishes and then stood back.

Gus inspected his dish, next to him the cat was carefully looking over her offering. Then she stood back while Gus came over to see what she had on offer.

Gus decided it was his day for fish, so the cat, judging it was wiser not to try sharing, started on his meat. It found favour.

Coffin stared down at them. I don't know what it is with you two, he said to himself, but when Stella feeds you then you eat what she gives you, when I put it out, you move around. I think you are passing judgement on me, not the food.

'Watch yourself, you two. Mind your manners or I will report you to the boss. She knows how to see you behave yourselves.'

After a while, the cat moved away from the dog's dinner, leaving it half finished. She gave Coffin an indifferent stare, then sat down to wash her face and paws. Presently Gus, a fast eater, finished the fish and turned his attention to what was left of his own meal which he despatched efficiently.

Coffin found it was relaxing and soothing talking to the animals who didn't care a damn for bloody guts inside tins, except possibly as food, but even this he doubted. Both of them liked their meals carefully and delicately presented to them. Stella had indulged them, no doubt about it.

'She'll be home soon,' he said hopefully, 'I ought to keep a watch on you two,' he said, stroking the cat's head. 'Time we gave you a name. Angel no longer seems right. But I reckon you like being anonymous.' He missed Stella and he didn't mind who knew it. No telephone call last night as promised, and when he'd called her mobile, no answer came there. Oh, she'd ring, of course she would, Stella wasn't the sort to disappear without a word. Nor did she approve of people who said they would telephone and then did not. Theatrical people suffered enough from that anyway. So did the police, thought Coffin as he walked away from the animals to make himself some tea.

Of course, sometimes it went the other way and you got calls you didn't want instead. Like the man who had been ringing up lately and saying he'd heard about the paedophile photographs and it was the police sending them to themselves.

Coffin sat at the kitchen table to drink his tea. The kitchen was half way up the winding stair, and he had come straight up there with the animals following him for their meal. Without Stella, he did not feel like penetrating further into his house. He had even been sleeping in the flat which the Chief Commander could use at will on the top floor of the police building. This was a plain but efficient set of rooms, always clean and tidy and ready for his use.

The young cat was now sitting on the windowsill. She turned to look at Coffin, then leapt to the floor.

'Oh don't say it. You want to go out.'

The cat was already moving.

'Can't you go out through the kitchen window?'

It was a rhetorical question: in the first place, the young cat could not answer, and secondly, it was going down the staircase fast.

Coffin stumped down the stairs after him. Since his home was in an old church tower, it was a complex of staircases and oddly placed little corridors. He was fond of the cat, he liked all cats, but missing Stella made him irritable. No sign of Gus, but he had a way of disappearing until it suited him to show his furry face again.

But there was Gus at the foot of the stairs, looking up at him. He made a noise somewhere between a bark and a growl.

'What's up, Gus?'

Then he saw the figure lying, face down, on the corridor floor.

'Stella... my God, Stella.'

A bent and twisted arm lay at her side.

He had seen horrible sights enough in his time, but nothing had pierced his heart and guts like this.

Gus moved towards the arm, to sniff,

'No, no, Gus, don't. Don't touch.'

Then he steadied himself.

* * *

'Good thing I telephoned,' said Stella, her voice clear and strong.

She was talking to Coffin later that day, late at night, after her day's filming. He was in their own sitting room in the tower of St Luke's drinking some claret.

'I've been trying to telephone you for hours.' He had not had a good day, he had been frightened and made a fool of over the mock body.

And there was a new horror which, at the moment, only he knew of.

'Only to tell me I was dead...'

Coffin could pick up the hint of amusement. 'Only because it was you.' he said hotly. It had not been funny. 'Or was pretending to be you. Plastic or some imitation. Pretty old and work-used mannequin.'

'Oh thanks.'

Coffin ignored this. 'Forensics have taken it away to check.'

'I hope it wasn't wearing any of my clothes.'

'I don't think so.' About this he could not be sure, but they had not looked the quality of clothes that Stella wore.

'And how did the pseudo me get into the house?'

'Through a small door at the side. It is locked, of course, but doesn't have all the security of the other door.'

'That's because it's left for whoever is looking after Gus to get in and out for him and with him as necessary.'

She didn't sound in the least alarmed, but that was because he had not told her about the stalker business. Also because once, early in their relationship, she had said: I know you'll always look after me. She probably still believed it.

They looked after each other, of course, and sometimes he guessed he needed it the more. He never got used to the really horrifying details of some murders, although he had learnt not to show it.

'Any post?' she asked.

'Er... No,' said Coffin. No need to tell her yet of the parcel dripping with blood. Later he would have to question her, just in case she could suggest a sender and a motive. 'Might be a few bills. Why?' He thought he detected a nuance in her voice that made him want an answer.

'No deliveries?'

'Were you expecting anything?' he prevaricated.

'I had a kind of a bill here.'

'In Edinburgh?' He couldn't keep the surprise out of his voice.

'Yes,' said Stella sharply. 'It's not on the moon, you know.'

'All right, all right. Apologies to Scotland.'

'Oh you're such an old Londoner.'

She was talking away because she didn't want to tell him about the bill received. They both knew it.

'Come on, Stella. It's this bill, I want to know. And you want to tell me, love, so don't dilly dally.'

Slowly, she said: 'It called itself an invoice...said it was for the delivery of a parcel and that I would receive the bill.'

'What was named in the invoice?' Coffin asked.

'Didn't say. Nor the price. Funny invoice, I thought.'

Funny altogether, thought Coffin.'

'Have I had a parcel?'

He was going to have to tell her, but not now, not over the telephone. 'I will find out and let you know. But you will be home tomorrow.'

There was a pause. 'As bad as that? One of those things that I have to see with my own eyes.'

'Not quite... it's in the forensic lab at the moment.'

'So I won't even see it?'

'Better not.'

Coffin realised he would have to tell Stella something of what was in the tin box, blood and all. He told her briefly.

Stella received it with some calm, but then she had not seen the offering, Coffin reflected.

'A nice present,' she said.

He would like to have said 'Nothing personal', but the figure dropped in their home suggested it was. 'It's part of a wider affair that is under investigation,' he said. Publicity about the paedophile case had been discouraged.

'The murders of the girls?' asked Stella.

'Oh, you've read about them?'

'Of course, it's not the moon up here as I just pointed out. The sins and violence of the Second City of London are dwelt upon with enthusiasm in Edinburgh and places north,' said Stella.

There was worse, but he was not going to tell her about the other victim.

'As things are it's not easy to know what is connected with what, and what fits in where,' he said honestly.

'I bet you've got a feeling,' said Stella, who knew her man.

'Then you also know that feelings can be wrong.'

'Yes, but I also now that those feelings that turn out to be wrong, can lead you to the answer. Underneath they can sometimes have a sort of truth.'

'How did the show go?' said Coffin to change the subject. When Stella became philosophical it was often the beginning of a quarrel.

'Oh pretty good, 'said Stella, willingly diverted to her own interests. 'I don't think it will go to a second series but my part was a beaut and there were hints of another home for it... a development of it built entirely around my part... I am to be a kind of modern witch.'

'You will play it beautifully, my darling.'

Stella considered this, decided not to take offence, he might have said 'naturally' and in certain moods might have done upon which she would have felt bound to show irritation, even anger, but he had not said it, so she said it herself.

'Naturally.'

And then they both laughed. Their marriage was based on laughter rather than anger. Marriages could be built on anger, she knew that too. Look at the Macbeths... that was anger all right.

'What are you laughing at?' demanded Coffin.

'I was feeling glad you weren't King Macbeth.'

'Quite glad myself. '

'I'm flying down tomorrow.'

'I'll send a car to Heathrow.'

He would not go himself: he knew he had another duty. Superintendent Miller and Inspector Winnie Ardet had told him that they wanted him to see the body of the latest murdered victim; and that he then might want to see where the body had been found.

He considered the message from Jack Miller and Winnie Ardet which Paul Masters had recorded and passed on.

Coffin had an uneasy feeling that a ghost was walking.

'Superintendent Miller rang,' Paul Masters said. 'He wanted to talk to you himself, but of course, you were at the committee meeting in Whitehall.'

'And a waste of time that was.'

Paul had come into Coffin's office to talk over a cup of coffee, carefully brewed by Paul himself from the best Mocha. The two men had an easy relationship. Paul was as neatly and even elegantly dressed as usual but in contrast when you saw him at his desk, he would peer at you out of a mountain of files and folders. He knew his way through it all but few others would.

'Miller really wants to talk to you.'

'And for me to see today's victim.' The fourth, not yet named.

Paul nodded.

'Jack Miller can be a tricky bastard,' said Coffin, pouring whisky into his coffee.

Paul looked thoughtful. He usually pretended not to hear when the Chief Commander let slip a criticism of a fellow officer.

Coffin added hastily: 'He doesn't usually want his hand held though.'

'I'm sorry it means you can't meet Miss Pinero off the flight.'

Coffin drained his coffee. 'Well, wheel them in when they arrive. I take it that Winnie Ardet is coming too?'

'Oh yes, she rang me up herself.' Something in his voice made Coffin give him a sharp look. 'I will see you have everything necessary so you are well briefed, sir.'

When you are dealing with the likes of Jack Miller it is good to be well prepared, Paul Masters was right enough there, so Coffin had the files on the earlier murders sent to him.

He sat studying them.

First: Amy Buckly.

Second: Mary Rice,

Third: Phillida Jessup, name just established. Still to be confirmed.

Now a fourth girl, so far name unknown.

One thing all the deaths had in common, apart from the method of murder and the rape, was that they took place in the district of Spinnergate.

It was not like Jack Miller to show much emotion. Coffin had thought that he had trained himself to regard victims as non-people, (although he was reputed to be a good family man and loving husband, fond of dogs too), but this case must be different.

Amy Buckly had been found by the Close Canal, an eighteenth century construction which still carried barge traffic today. Her body was stretched, face down, in the mud and weeds on a narrow path which bordered the canal. She had been dead about six hours. Aged twenty-four, she was a school teacher who had taught a class of some twenty infants in Close Street School. She had been a pretty girl. Her Jack Russell dog had been with her on that last walk by the canal, one they often took together, so Coffin was told, and it was his return home alone to where she lived with her family that started the search. She was found by a woman police constable who had been at school with Amy.

Ten days later, Mary Rice was found dead near the railway station she used to travel into central London every day to work in an office, where she had a job in IT. She was in her late twenties. She often stayed late in London after work to eat with friends, perhaps have a drink, and then come home. She had a small flat, sometimes shared with a boyfriend, sometimes alone. Currently, she had been on her own. Her body was tucked away in an alley behind the railway station where it had been found by a man going on early shift the next morning. She had been dead about five hours.

Phillida Jessup had died just a couple of days after Mary Rice, although her body had not been found so soon. It was finally discovered on Pilling Common, a notorious place of death. She was the youngest of the three victims, a student at the local university in her first year reading for a language degree. Her body had been found in the University Botanical Gardens. Her father was a CID officer in the London Met.

When Coffin read that he wondered if this was why Jack Miller was anxious to see him.

He was just considering that, and turning his eyes towards the folder on the latest victim who had also been found on

Pilling Common, though not near where Phillida Jessup had turned up, when Jack Miller and Winnie Ardet arrived.

Ever the gentleman, Superintendant Miller let Winnie walk in first. Winnie managed her usual smile but both officers looked worried.

'Thanks for seeing us so soon, sir,' said Miller.

'Serial killings have a horror of their own,' said Coffin with sympathy. 'And you *are* sure that this is what you are handling?'

'Oh it's one man all right,' said Miller gloomily. 'And a cunning one too... even if we cop him we might have a job pinning it on him. He leaves none of his blood or semen around. Pity he didn't start operating in the Met. area. Why us in the Second City?'

'Lives or works here?' said Coffin, making it a question.

'Not hard to get here to do the work,' said Winnie. 'Could start from anywhere. That's what I think. So far, we have no evidence.'

'Certainly knows the district,' said Jack Miller. 'I wish he had kept out of Spinnergate. Seems keen on Pilling Common, but he isn't the first. Probably not the last. '

'Could be one of a ring of friendly faces looking at us, and we don't know. That's what's worrying us and what we wanted to say.' This was Winnie Ardet at her most earnest. She went on: 'We are terribly anxious.'

Coffin felt he had worries of his own that were being passed over. Did they not know?

They must have heard on the excellent police communication network of the paedophile investigation, impossible that they shouldn't, but nothing was said.

They had heard, of course, but were not mentioning it. Or not yet. Perhaps it was called tact.

'The reason we need to speak to you, sir, is that there are tales, rumours floating round that the murderer is a police officer. Either acting or retired. Everyone has picked it up. Have you, sir?'

'No, nothing has come my way.' Not officially but hints and murmurs.

'And the twist to the tale is,' said Jack Miller fiercely, 'the extra bit of sauce is that the rumour has it that the man is someone I know. No one is willing to offer a name, of course,' he ended savagely.

Coffin shook his head.

'I bet Paul Masters has heard something,' said Miller. 'So I want to go at him.'

'I guess Masters would have told me and quite soon too, if he thought it important. ' But he knows this paedophile thing oppresses me. 'Anyway, let's have him in and ask. '

Paul Masters answered the summons, nodded his head and admitted yes, stories had been coming to him. 'I would have told you, of course sir, if it had been anything but rumour. No names, of course. Nothing you can lay hands on. My feeling is that it's a bit of nastiness with no foundation, the sort that springs up sometimes. Anything concrete would have come to you at once.'

'Good.' He turned to Superintendent Miller and Inspector Ardet. 'So I am not going to hand the case over to the Met. and ask you two to retire from the case which I guess was what you came to do. '

There was a silence. 'We'll get him, sir,' said Miller fiercely. 'Thank you for your confidence.' Then he said: 'Heard about the paedophile you've got... Glad to help if we could.'

'Thank you.'

'I wondered if you would come to see the latest victim. No name yet.'

'Do you think I might know her?'

'There's a chance, sir, she had a newspaper in her pocket with an article about the killings, your name was mentioned, and she had ringed it round.... Doesn't mean anything, of course, sir, but we are trying every angle.'

He looked at his diary, then at his watch. He had less than an hour free. 'Let's do it then, let's do it now.'

Nothing could make Coffin take these visits to see a body in the police mortuary in his stride. It was death, and not usually a peaceful one. True, this was one of the duties from which rising importance had emancipated him, and he usually managed to avoid it. So why was he going now?

Because he was asked. What better reason?

Now as he looked down at the small figure, he thought that the dead always appear to shrink. At first, anyway.

Miller peeled back the sheet over the face.

He looked in silence. 'Yes, I do know her. Or I did.' He turned away more moved than he wanted to show. 'She was my secretary, a temporary one, a few years ago. Poor child.'

She had been young, and now somehow looked even younger in death.

He hoped he would not have to reveal that she had developed a kind of love for Coffin and that was why he had had to dismiss her. Or move her on; the word dismissal had not been mentioned.

'At least I can give you her name, Angela Dover, and Paul Masters will be able to give addresses and so on.'

I must get to Masters first, he thought, warn him. But Paul was always discreet.

Coffin was beginning to have an uneasy feeling that the two serious cases, the murders and the paedophile were bumping into each other more and more.

Is there a connection? he asked himself.

Only in time and space, in his memory of other cases.

Life was not as straightforward and easy for the Chief Commander as it might have been. Before he could speak to Paul Masters, he had to take several telephone calls, firstly three recorded messages. He plugged the earpiece in so he could hear and no one else could listen in.

The first, which he welcomed, was from Stella. 'Hello, love. On my way home, I'm at Edinburgh airport, hoping to catch the next flight. Haven't booked a seat, but I think I'll get on.

Hopefully, as they say. Don't even try to meet me... I bet you weren't anyway, I think I told you not to, but I can see Jamesy Davy and he always has his Rolls to meet him, show off that he is, so I will get him to bring me home.' Of course he was not jealous of Jamesy who had nothing except his looks and a certain acting skill, but what would they do with him when they got him? Take him out to dinner and wish him well? Stella did not wait for him to answer before it was Goodbye Love, and she was gone, so no decision was demanded of him.

The next call was different. It came from a friend and former colleague in the Met., Commander Peter Barnes.

'Pete here, sorry not to speak to you in person but I have to get off and you have your answerphone on permanently as far as I can see.'

This was true enough. Except for calls routed through Paul Masters which Coffin took after consideration, all calls to his office were recorded. You could get him at home. If you were lucky. (Stella had her own phone and own number... essential, she claimed in her business. Anyway, most people used her mobile or sent her email messages.)

'There is a rumour going round that your Stella has a stalker after her. If this is true, it may be the same one who had a trial run here in South London last year. Used to send presents of a nasty kind with the threat of more to follow. Never caught. We thought we had him, but no. Moved on? Could it be your fellow or an imitator? Let's meet and talk. Advice: Don't tell Stella... he's looking for fear as a prize.'

The third call was nothing but silence, with the hint of a distant laugh. A giggle... Somehow that was less agreeable.

Working with Paul Masters on routine affairs, Coffin asked: 'Any idea who would ring up and just giggle...?'

'Always a few lunatics around,' said Masters lightly, as he handed over a file of letters to be signed.

Not very cheering, thought Coffin, even as he admitted the truth of it.

'Check where the call came from,' he ordered.

The answer soon came back: number withheld.

Phoebe who had appointed herself as Gus-Looker-After had given the dog a walk and returned him to his master, where he was now sitting on the Chief Commander's feet. Dog and man, left alone, both considered Stella's return.

'She won't be long now, old chap.'

Phoebe Astley telephoned to confirm that, as from this moment, she had taken over the paedophile operation. 'No progress as yet'. What a beast the man is. Is he one person or group? What could you call him, she asked herself -- a deranged paedophile stalker? Something to find out. Also does he buy photographs or did he take them all himself? She well knew there were outfits that specialised in marketing paedophilia. No, she thought they were purchased, the pictures varied in style so much. A lot to find out here.

Coffin went back to his desk work where presently Paul Masters came in to ask him if he would take a call from Commander Peter Barnes.

Again? thought Coffin. Twice in one day?

'Put him through.'

He knew at once, from Pete Barnes' voice that it was not good news.

'Stella with you?'

'No, she's not back yet. ' He did not want to ask, but he had to. ' Why?'

'One of my mates in Scotland had an anonymous call saying that the Stalker had got her.'

There was a long, long dark night ahead for Coffin.

To his furious and alarmed shout at Pete Barnes (and he was not a shouter) demanding evidence, he got the answer that a fax had come through, Stella's terrified face, and on it typed: Look to the Lady. It had been sent to the hotel where Stella had been staying.

'The hotel passed the fax on at once to the local police... they are well informed, knew what was going on in the Second City, and certainly knew who Stella is. I have a mate there, and he saw I had a copy fast,' Barnes said. He had started to say 'was' but hurriedly altered it to the present tense, at no time would he be the one to push Stella into the past.

When the fax arrived on Coffin's desk he looked at it and felt sick. Then he looked again. Then he looked again.

'This fax,' he said, 'is of a picture of Stella in a film, made some years ago too. This is Stella acting, not Stella here and now.'

'It's a calling card,' said Pete with relief in his voice.

'But also a warning.'

As far as could be established Stella had caught her flight from Edinburgh, the flight had arrived safely but she had not telephoned her husband. She had left the hotel in Scotland where she had been staying, saying goodbye and that she was off home, and that was the last her friends had seen of her.

'Trace where the fax came from,' ordered Coffin, praying that his wife would arrive at any moment, surprised at how very anxious he was. Spouses of important officers did get such messages sometimes.

Phoebe Astley's office had also received the same fax. But it had only been given attention much later than the one sent to Fillmore on the edge of Edinburgh, from which Commander Peter Barnes' friend had passed it on. For this Phoebe was apologetic. Coffin accepted her apology; he knew well that not all faxes get prompt attention. One of the facts of life.

Phoebe herself was horrified at what had happened. Or, in this case, not happened. 'Such a mass of faxes has come through, it was kind of imbedded in them.'

'Find out where the fax came from,' ordered Coffin once again.

'Ought not to be difficult. Comes over the telephone wire, after all.'

'And get hold of James Davy, that actor, Stella said he would give her a lift in his car from Heathrow.'

'I'll call on him myself, sir.' There was a reserved note in Phoebe's voice. 'He's so beautiful, isn't he? And that lovely voice. I'll take someone with me.'

Coffin wanted to say: Oh don't worry, he's more likely to seduce his chauffeur than you, but he contented himself with 'Thank you.'

No one's virtue was tried one way or another as it soon transpired that James had not gone to London but stayed in Scotland, travelling to Pitlochry to see a friend who was in a play there. He was obliging his chauffeur to drive north to collect him.

'Just like Jamie, ' thought Coffin, 'putting himself first. If he'd been on that flight, he could have looked after Stella.'

Coffin found that his misery worked in two strands: in one he could make bitter jokes about people like James Davy, while in the other, he was sure he would never know happiness again.

The long dark night wore on.

Coffin went between his home in the tower and his office, hoping for a message or the sight of Stella in either. He drank a great deal of coffee but thought it wiser not to go for the whisky because when Stella did appear he wanted to be sober.

Stella *must* appear.

Paul Masters came in during the night with the information that the London fax had been sent from: 'Mind Machine in Ely Street, Spinnergate. One of those outfits with rows of computers, printers and faxes.'

'It would be Spinnergate,' said Coffin, who felt he hated Spinnergate. Oh God, where was Stella? A search was going on, but so far, nothing, 'Not near Minden Street? They had had their own Jack the Ripper there.'

'Near Madras Market.'

'Near enough,' said Coffin gloomily for whom it was becoming a bad night. A bad bloody night.
It was a bad night for Phoebe too.

She had also been given some news in the night... and it wasn't good news. She did not know why it had come to her, she was not dealing with the murders. Except she did know: that bloody fax with 'Look to the Lady' on it.

She knew she must wait for morning before telling Coffin. 'We have a body. A woman, not long dead. Badly cut up.'

She could not tell the Chief Commander straight away. She must see the body first to see if it was Stella.

Chapter 4

The man, so falsely called a stalker (murderer of women he might be, collector of odds and ends of bodies he might also be, but stalker he was not) considered his official description as he went to his wardrobe.

He knew what a stalker was in the police sense, none better, but he rejected the description. Being a careful reader of the newspapers and also wanting to know what was said of his exploits, he had read that he was so named.

He grinned. A stalker moved with careful, quiet tread after his innocent, nervous prey. Now that was not his approach. Imagination, style, was his mark. More of an actor. Or actress, a sex label was not important. He went to his wardrobe to choose what to wear today. Or tonight as it would be.

No, library first, then the costume. Inspiration before execution.

Catch them when they are not thinking.

He opened a drawer in a chest of four drawers. He called it a library but it was more properly a collection: a collection of drawings and photographs. Not one of the pictures therein was his work, but his was the pleasure. After all, the hand that enjoys the glitter of the diamond had not dug, cut, or polished the gem, just paid a price and got the satisfaction.

I am a complicated person, he told himself, studying a picture of a child. In fact, I am not one person but two, three even. No one really knows who I am.

Idly, death being much on his mind, he wondered which of his selves would die first. He would not have a choice, of course. Just depended what cap he had on. He would wear a hat, it was decidedly a head covering day. Or night, more precisely. He chose the cap from a selection he had built up, then adjusted it with care.

He happened to know that Stella Pinero was short sighted.

She might not recognise his face, but she would certainly recognise what he was wearing.

If she thought about it at all, she might wonder how he knew where to find her.

You're a very well known lady, Stella, here in the Second City, and your publicity people do a good job. Good job for me too, Stella. So when I read in the gossip column in the local newspaper that you were finishing up the filming in Scotland, this week, day named, and that you planned to grab the first plane back, I knew what to do.

Watch for you on the last two flights of the day. Don't see you being earlier. In fact, I would have taken a bet on it being the last flight. I rate you, emotionally, a last plane of the day woman.

There was a picture of you too in the paper so I knew you had a new hair cut, a new colour too for all I knew. I would know you though, Miss Pinero, Lady Coffin.

* * *

Stella arrived, tired but cheerful at Heathrow airport. She didn't expect to be met so she was walking briskly to the taxi rank, when a voice halted her.

'Ma'am, Lady Coffin, Miss Pinero... PC Waters, the Chief Commander asked me to meet you...'

Stella looked at him. 'So my husband sent you?'

The man nodded. Not a talkative type Stella decided. 'Are you a police officer?'

'Retired, ma'am. I used to be PC Waters... now I have my own business'. He held the car door open. The cap pulled down over his forehead, dark spectacles , and handkerchief up to his nose. A huge sneeze.

'Sorry, ma'am, nothing catching. Just hay fever.'

'Don't know you, do I?'

'You've forgotten me, ma'am.' He was handing her towards the car.

Stella was tired, content for the moment to lie back and let the streets of London slip past her. It was a dark quiet night, the time when she most liked the city. She felt its history then with a sense of the small, ancient villages which had been absorbed into the docklands. Her husband had said that he was convinced that some of the local slang was Anglo-Saxon in origin, if not earlier still, Celtic. 'Mind you,' he had added with a laugh, 'most of the words that have come through couldn't be called dinner table talk.'

For a minute or two she dozed, letting the familiar streets slip past. She had had almost nothing to eat all day, working hard to get finished, but she had shared a bottle of champagne with a few of the cast. It had not been very good champagne which distantly, dreamily, she began to blame for the weird dreams that tramped through her head. She saw strange pictures of strings of blood, ribbons of blood. Distantly, she heard a voice calling her name. Not a voice she knew. Then the picture in her head went dark and then darker still. Shapes, figures in this darkness. Silent. Voiceless.

But the sleep was not deep and soon she came to the surface. She looked out of the window but did not recognise the road. On either side were tall, neglected buildings, which looked empty. Old disused factories which had not yet been converted into smart apartments. Possibly never would be, she thought. Not where she would choose to live.

This wasn't the way home.

She leaned forward and tapped the driver on the shoulder. 'You've taken the wrong route.'

Close to, she thought that she did not care for the look of the back of his neck. You could tell a lot from a man's neck, she thought: this was a thick, unlovely neck which did not suggest a good person. He was wearing an old raincoat pulled up high.

He did not answer her but began to slow down while drawing into the kerb. Hell is a city much like London, she thought suddenly. Marvellous Shelley. She had a strong unexpected feeling that the sooner she was out of the cab the better. Stella started to open the cab door, meaning to get out. Then she would find out the name of the road and ask the way of the first pedestrian she met. As far as she could see at the moment the road was empty. It was late, probably about midnight by now. Certainly felt late.

But before she could do so, a tall, thin figure began to get in the car. Another man, she thought.

'What is this? Who are you? Driver, what's going on?'

He turned his head towards her, looking over his shoulder, eyes still masked with dark spectacles.

'Sometimes it is better to hunt in pairs.' His teeth showed in a grin.

At this point Stella realised with a shock that the second figure, masked and impossible to identify, was probably a woman.

Chapter 5

Coffin awoke with a feeling of heavy pressure on his stomach. Without opening his eyes he knew that this came from Gus seeking comfort and company.

'He must have put on weight,' thought Coffin sleepily. But no, lying on top of the dog, completely relaxed and at ease, was the ginger cat. The pair, after a first period of cautious hostility, had adopted a cautious friendship. Or it might be fairer to say that the cat made the advances and Gus put up with it. Perhaps it was not true to say that Gus had a kind heart, but he was a polite fellow.

Coffin was still half asleep but he woke up with a start.

Stella... where was Stella?

He sat up with a jerk, dislodging both the animals. Of course he wasn't in bed, you don't go comfortably to bed when your beloved wife is missing. He was lying on top of the covers with a blanket thrown over him. He didn't remember even getting that far himself, and it was possible that Phoebe or Paul Masters had led or pushed him that way as exhaustion grew too great to fight off. There was a mug of coffee or tea on the bed table, but he could tell by the skin on the top that it had been there a long time. All night, probably, he didn't remember putting it there.

It was morning. A grey, grim daylight was flooding the room. He could hear rain beating against the window.

Oh Stella, Stella, where are you?

Then the telephone by the bed began to ring. He reached out, dislodging the cat who was sitting there looking at him, then knocking over the mug of coffee as he went.

As his hand touched the phone, it stopped ringing. The instrument was wet with cold coffee.

'Damn you,' he said to the cat who gave him a green-eyed stare in return.

His hand shaking, he dialled the code which allowed you to learn which number had just called. In reply all he got was a taped, tinny voice telling him that the caller rang from a public call box and the number was therefore unavailable.

Coffin slammed the receiver down then got out of bed. Coldly, fiercely he began to telephone Phoebe Astley.

The events of the day before began awakening in his mind, coming alive before his eyes and ears.

First, a happy call from Stella saying that she was on her way home.

Then followed, far too quickly, by the message about Stella saying that the Stalker had got her.

'I didn't believe it,' said Coffin aloud. 'No one did.' But Stella had arrived on the flight from Scotland and had not been seen since.

Yesterday he had got down to his routine of work, completing a report, answering letters, while inside a fury of anxiety and anger fought with each other. The anger touched Phoebe Astley and Paul Masters, both of whom understood and forgave without showing either of those emotions which would certainly have angered Coffin even more. He was frustrated with himself and sometimes felt a flash of anger at Stella.

The telephone rang again. This time it was Phoebe.

It's not Stella,' she said at once to him. 'But I would like you to take a look at a body.'

'So you think it *is* her,' he said savagely.

She was silent for a moment. 'I just want to make sure, sir - I thought...'

'Thank you, Phoebe,' said Coffin, not altogether kindly. 'You thought that once I had seen this latest poor, dead, ravaged creature and saw it wasn't Stella that I would walk away in relief. Well, I don't think I will, I think I will just know what my wife could look like when it has been her turn.'

'All the same, I would be pleased if you'd come to look at the dead woman,' said Phoebe steadily. 'I'll drive.'

'No, you won't drive, and neither will I. I will take the official car which I use when I want to look important.'

Phoebe nodded, accepting her fate (which at the moment clearly was to irritate the Chief Commander) and went to wait for the car. She knew from past experience that the official car, so called, unless ordered well in advance, could take its time about arriving. Coffin rarely used it, preferring to drive himself. She remembered him telling her once that as a young and hard-up detective in South London he had seen one of what he called 'the boss figures' driving past in an official car, and he had fantasised about the pleasures of such a car and had promised he would have the right to one himself in time. There was something sad, and yet typical of him, that now he had it, he did not care for it.

Then she rallied: don't underestimate him you've known him long enough to know how tough and resilient he is.

Stella too, she reassured herself. Whatever pool Stella falls into, you can back her to rise to the top and climb out. You had to *find* the pool first though, came the reminder, and while every police unit in London and beyond had been alerted, no sighting of Stella had come through. Nothing to suggest where further inquiry might be useful. What the police called a 'black silence' was operating. Could be broken at any moment, of course, but all you could do at the now was pray if you were that way inclined, or swear if that was more your style.

She did both.

'Come on, Stella, surface,' she found herself saying, then adding without meaning to: Dead or Alive.

Phoebe got into the car after the Chief Commander, then the two of them sat in the back in silence.

'The last time I did a visit like this I recognised the victim, Angela Dover, and she had worked for me once,' said Coffin. 'Did that help at all?'

Phoebe said in a thoughtful voice. 'As you know Jack Miller is handling the murders, but I can tell you something about Angela Dover, she was a great clubber. Out every night to various places, dancing, drinking, drugs as well possibly. She was quite a wild one. She could easily have attracted the notice of the killer.'

'She looked such a quiet girl,' said Coffin.

'Oh, looked.' Phoebe shrugged.

'I could do with a result.'

'There's a lot of effort going into the killings and the paedophile letters as well,' said Phoebe, evasively.

'In other words, no progress? In spite of Angela? Poor Angela, not even helping towards a solution. Am I right?'

'Not quite, sir. You know yourself there can be negative progress when wrong ideas are ruled out, and on the positive side, every little bit of information counts.'

'Faxes, phone calls: this chap is using them and getting away, laughing.'

'In the end, they will *give* us an answer.'

'You mean someone will come rushing in and shout: I know who it is, the killer is John Bloggs of Brown Street.'

'Yes,' said Phoebe, doggedly. 'And it very likely might be you, sir, you know how to get results.'

'He knows me and he knows Stella, this killer and the paedophile, I know they're connected' said Coffin. 'That I swear.'

'You are a public figure, and so is Stella.'

The Chief Commander got out of the car. 'Wait for us, Norris.'

'Of course, sir.' Norris was holding the car door. Norris had been a black cab driver before coming to the Second City and he always drove the police car as if it was a Rolls.

Feeling desolate, longing for the telephone in his pocket to ring and to hear the voice of Stella, Coffin turned to Phoebe.

'Come on then. Let's get this over.'

As he looked down at the poor, carved up body of another young woman, he wanted to say: 'Just more of the same,' but he couldn't do it because every death was both the same and yet different. You owed it to the dead to admit this.

In fact, this woman had been dead longer than Stella had been absent. It was not a new killing.

'I don't know this poor creature. You rate her as one of the series? Not just a victim flung in by someone else as an extra?'

Phoebe shook her head. 'No, both the pathologist and the forensic team assert that she was killed by the same pair of hands.'

The naked body, swollen and with patches of discoloration, also bore a savage knife cut out which supported this assertion. 'Where was she found?'

'In an alley way off behind an old factory in Spinnerwick.' Phoebe did not add that the knowledgable Mimsie Marker (who had somehow found out about the body before any public announcement) had told her that Pepper Alley was a well known place for the tucking away of awkward bodies and that this was the third or so in Mimsie's memory. 'Makes him a local, dear, doesn't it?' she had said, handing over her morning paper to DCI Astley.

'The pathologist, Dr. Hair - no one you know, sir - says that the distribution and demarcation of florid hypostasis on the front of the breasts and abdomen indicates that she had been in a cramped position and the body doubled up for a number of hours in a confined space... a cupboard or a car boot.'

'Helpful if either the car or the cupboard can be located.' Without another word, Phoebe nodded at the mortuary attendant who had been standing watching them. He lifted one leg so that Coffin could see the back of the dead woman's calf.

'The pathologist thought that possibly more than one person was involved in the killing.'

'What makes him think that?' Coffin was not entirely convinced.

'There are bruises on her arms and legs: the placing and size and shape of which he does not believe could come from *one* pair of hands.'

'Any chance of the odd fingerprint showing up?' Coffin knew that in certain circumstances this could be so. A bloody fingerprint could always be read.

DCI Astley knew what he was thinking, but no luck. 'Not a fingerprint, although there is some blood.'

'Two people, two killers,' said Coffin as he turned away. 'Have there been two all the time and we didn't notice?'

'It's possible, isn't it?'

'Are you telling me that Stella is in the hands of two men?'

'I can't possibly know that, sir. It's just something that seemed indicated and I thought I ought to tell you.' Phoebe made her voice more determined. 'We will find her.' She put an emphasis on every word.

'Oh thank you...' But he knew he was being unfair. 'I feel that I ought to be out pounding the streets looking for her.' He turned to the attendant. 'Cover her up.'

Phoebe led him outside. 'Have a good scream.'

To her relief, the Chief Commander laughed. 'Not quite my style.'

'It's a relief, I can tell you.'

'I don't believe you have ever done it.' Coffin looked at the self contained, controlled face of the Chief Inspector.

'Haven't I though. You don't know the world I live in , sir.'

Coffin thought he did, and better than Phoebe Astley understood, but he took himself quietly back to his office, hoping against hope that Stella would greet him. All the time, he was haunted by a picture of her lying dead in a field , by a hedge, covered up with leaves and branches.

He had walked back to his office, leaving Phoebe behind with the car. In the outer office, Paul Masters was huddled over a set of documents. He looked up and said good morning but before he could say more an assistant hurried forward with a parcel.

'This came for you, sir.'

'Why haven't you opened it?'

'It's marked personal, Chief Commander.'

'We don't usually take much notice of that.' He reached out his hand for a neat brown paper parcel. 'Cut the string for me.' He was suspicious. 'Don't leave any fingerprints on it.'

'It's such pretty stuff: red and blue,' said his helper, but she did cut it. The paper unfolded delicately as if on purpose to show what was inside.

It was a shoe.

'I think it is Stella's,' said Coffin. His voice was unsteady.

'But why is there only one?' The assistant seemed puzzled.

Coffin did not answer, and Paul Masters, who had been watching and listening unobtrusively, got up and called the woman away. 'Marge, come and give me a hand. I want help.'

'Thanks,' muttered Coffin. He looked at Marge and could almost see the half joke forming in her mind, but thank God, not on her lips: And has Lady Coffin only got one leg?

But what she actually said, with a cry of surprise...'Oh sir, there's blood.'

Coffin thought to himself that it was a *coup de foudre*. He got Phoebe on the phone immediately. 'I want more officers on this, it's essential we find Stella before it's too late.'

With difficulty, Coffin finished his day's routine of work. He had a talk on the telephone with the Head of CID in London, in which they settled the arrangements for a meeting later in the month. He said nothing about Stella but he thought the man knew from the way he asked after her. Then he composed some reports, read one or two others and censored another couple. All work which required just enough mental effort to keep the top of his mind occupied while his worry for Stella rumbled underneath.

He really thought that was the end of his paperwork for the time being so he slipped home to see to the animals. There was another packet waiting. He flinched from opening it but it had to be done.

Inside using a dog, and horse and a human female child

was one of the nastiest pieces of photographic pornography he had ever seen.

A slip of paper inside said: Do you want to join in, Stella?

He would like to have burnt it but being a policeman he was trained to keep the evidence so he put it in an envelope and sent it off to Dr James Carmichael (nicknamed Croggy) in the Dept of Practical Forensics who was making a careful study of all the pornographic material that had come in. He hoped to be able to draw some useful conclusions.

Coffin despatched the envelope, then came back to sit in his big chair by the window in his workroom to do something, anything. He did not expect to sleep but he was soon in a dream world.

In this dream world, which was not quite sleep, Stella and the mannequin walked together, hand in hand.

Chapter 6

While Coffin sat and wished he could sleep and dream, Dr Carmichael was working on the previous material sent him from Coffin's office. It was odious stuff but he was used to working on it and found it was smoothed down by numerous cups of tea and coffee. Stronger drinks he allowed himself as evening came on.

He hummed a cheerful tune as he worked. He really quite liked what he was doing but he did not admit it too readily because the material was so noisome. He had come to a certain conclusion about its origins (for they were various) and was pleased with himself.

'I shall tell the Chief Commander. I hope he will be pleased too. He ought to be. We make progress.'

'His Nibs is in fine fettle today,' said the senior of his two assistants to his junior.

'Perhaps he finds the stuff he's had to look at more amusing than he lets on.'

'No,' said the senior assistant, who had a great respect for Dr Carmichael, although not admitting to it. 'He's a very decent sort is old Carmichael. Laughing at those obscenities would not be his style at all. And he wouldn't like to see you laughing at them, and neither would I.'

'Don't worry, you won't.'

Paul Masters, who kept a protective eye on his boss (which fortunately Coffin had not noticed or nothing would have alarmed him more) telephoned Dr Carmichael who was an old friend. 'Hello, Croggy. How are things? That latest packet that I took the trouble to drop in straight off, anything of interest?'

Dr Carmichael was willing to chat. 'Join me in a drink and we'll talk. I have got something to say.'

'Where shall we meet?'

'What about the Archery Shed, just behind Mimsie Marker's stall?' Mimsie's stall, where she sold newspapers and magazines and refreshments, was famous in the Second City. It was near the busy tube station in Spinnergate down whose escalator the Chief Commander could often be seen hurrying on his way to London meetings.

In spite of its name, the Archery Shed knew no archers with bows but was a smart and expensive drinking spot where you could get good wine and food. The chic world of the Second City had discovered it (prompted thereto by Mimsie Marker who was reputed to own a share) and it was always crowded.

'I know where it is,' said Paul. 'See you there.' He was early but Dr Carmichael was already there before him, seated by the window, drinking chilled white wine and eating a smoked salmon sandwich.

'Looks expensive,' said Paul as he slid into a seat.

'It is, ' agreed Carmichael, 'but good.' He raised his hand to the waiter. 'I've ordered the same for you.'

'You're paying?' But he knew his friend.

'Of course not.' Dr Carmichael quaffed his wine. ' I've done a lot of work on pretty odious stuff for your lot.' He nodded his head. 'It's been interesting. I started off with no clear ideas of what was what. I never like to make up my mind in advance.'

Paul Masters nodded, this being all that was required of him.

'I suppose I took it for granted at first that the pictures came from one source. My experience is that the pornographer enjoys his own products beyond anyone else's. I mean it's kind of personal to them. But by degrees, I realised that there was no unity in this collection. I've got a much clearer idea of what has been going on: the chap who was collecting them and sending them on was interested in distressing the Chief Commander and Miss Pinero rather than giving himself pleasure. That's not usually the way of it.'

'I already got the idea that he didn't care for the Chief Commander and Lady Coffin very much.'

'All the same, it alters the picture.'

'I'll tell the Chief Commander what you say. Not that his mind will be on it until he gets Stella safe home again. Of course, he's got these serial murders on his mind too.'

'An obsessive paedophile and a serial killer, what a world,' said Dr Carmichael. 'Could they be connected? Who is handling the killings?'

'Superintendent Miller and Inspector Winnie Ardet. Phoebe Astley is handling the paedophile case... she took over when Joe Jones went out sick. She was working with Mercy Adams but Mercy is away too at the moment. But she'll be back.'

'Two good teams. I've had to work on a couple of the bodies, and let me tell you, they were not a pleasant job. There is something about them that reminds me of the paedophile's activities....' He stopped. 'Same man doing both perhaps... Do you know, I think I've said something important...'

'You might have done.' Paul knew that his friend never underestimated himself.

'Tell the Chief Commander, will you?'

'He might have thought of it for himself...Anyway, can I give you a lift home?

Paul Masters drove slowly through Spinnergate where the traffic was always heavy. He caught sight of a woman threading her way through the crowd on the opposite side of the road. He looked, then looked again.

'Is that Stella Pinero?'

Both men watched a slim figure hurrying along.

'I don't know,' said Dr Carmichael. 'Shall I get out of the car and go after her?'

'Yes, better had.'

They stopped the car, but by the time they were on the pavement, the woman had disappeared.

'It may have been her,' said Paul, 'but perhaps I'd better not say anything to the Chief.

Coffin fed the cat and dog once more, then sat back down in the big chair by the window in which he leaned back with closed eyes. He had not slept the night before because of thinking of Stella. Or that was what it felt like, but he thought he might have dreamt of her.

She had been gone for well over twenty-four hours now. He was constantly thinking of Stella. All the police teams were alerted to look for her, to report anything that was helpful. But there was nothing. Nothing.

Now he slept without realising it. When he opened his eyes there she was. Stella was standing, looking down at him.

'Stella, darling Stella, is it really you?' He stood up and put his arms round her; she was shivering slightly so that he held her tighter. 'What happened? Where were you?'

Stella took his hand, then sat down beside him. 'I'm glad to be back. I wasn't sure if I would make it.'

'Tell me everything. I'm so glad you're safe.'

'As to where I was, I was in a park, most of the time... I think, ' she added thoughtfully.

Coffin was silent for a moment, studying his wife's face. 'I believe you, my love, but why and how?'

'I got into a car you sent at Heathrow. Or I thought it was so. I was very tired and I'd had some champagne on the way home... only a glass or two, but I suppose it relaxed me. I went to sleep, just a doze... when I woke up - came round, it felt more like it- I didn't recognise the road... This isn't the way, I thought. I tapped the driver on the shoulder and told him it wasn't the way... then he turned round.'

Stella was silent. Then: 'I didn't like his face... I hadn't seen it properly before. And he did something... I can't remember exactly what it was now, but I didn't like it. But he slowed down so I opened the door to get out...then there was another man by this time.' She paused 'If it *was* a man.'

She paused again. 'Go on,' said Coffin.

'I pushed him or her back and jumped out...'

'I'm glad you did. And then?'

'He fell on the kerb, I remember that, then I think he jumped up and hit me, hit my head...' She gave her husband a smile. 'I'm vague about what happened next... I think I ran, I seem to remember running.'

There was a pause.

'The next thing I remember is waking up in a hut in a park. I must have run there. ' She shook her head. 'I must have dozed on and off for some time.' Most of the day it must have been really, but she was only just realising that fact. How odd. Was it shock or that champagne? Or the hard work she had done in Scotland? All acting together, perhaps.

'You are going to see a doctor,' said Coffin firmly.

'I'm never ill, ' Stella could be firm too.' Actresses are never ill, they can't afford to be.'

'No, I know that. But you had a blow to your head.'

'My feet hurt a bit but not my head.'

'Did you walk here?'

'I did. Once I worked out the way home... the park where I hid... not sure now why I hid, but it seemed distinctly the right thing to do at the time.'

'That was the blow on the head. You really must go to Dr Fielding... Or I will get him to come here.'

'No, I am going to have a bath and change. My memory is coming back and I know I have a script I must look at.'

Coffin watched his wife with concern but also admiration. You couldn't beat Stella. 'Would you be able to identify these two men?'

Stella considered. 'Don't know. I hope so. If I get the chance.'

She disappeared up the winding staircase for her bath, taking the cat with her for company. As soon as she had gone, the Chief Commander telephoned Paul Masters with the news that Stella was back. Masters thought it more tactful not to say that he had seen Stella. Nor did he say, although he knew he must soon, what Dr Carmichael thought of the collection of pictures.

'Thank God. What happened, what had she to say?'

'She was taken deliberately. Just chance and a great mercy that she got away. She'll have to make a statement. Tell Phoebe Astley, will you please? And set up some security for Stella.'

'Of course, I will.'

'And it better be good: I think the current serial killer wanted her for one of his victims. We've got to remember there was that dummy... that was aimed at Stella somehow.'

Abruptly, Paul Masters said: 'Dr Carmichael thinks the paedophile pictures are a put-together collection and he believes that they are also part of the murder investigation. The cases are connected.'

* * *

Later that evening, Superintendent Jack Miller and Inspector Winnie Ardet were having a coffee together. News got around and by this time, they had a pretty good idea of what had happened to Stella Pinero and were putting their own gloss on it.

'We have to tell the Chief Commmander our suspicions,' Winnie swigged her drink. 'Wonder what he'll make of it?'

'That's what we are sitting here discussing.' said Miller. 'He's a decent sort, he'll listen. Believe we've got it right, I think. Probably worked it out already. He's clever, you know.' He spoke with respect. 'It's all one case.'

'It deserves a place in the history of crime and murder,'

said Winnie Ardet, who had her academic side. 'I might write it myself.'

'We shall have to get an interview with Stella herself,' said Miller.

'Sure. I've always found her easy to talk to, haven't you? '

'How many murders have we had?'

'More than I care to count,' said Winnie, although she had counted and had set up the Incident room with many desks, one for every dead woman and another called Idea and Extras.

Amy Buckley
Mary Rice
Phillida Jessup
Angela Dover
The body in Pepper Alley as yet nameless.

And Stella Pinero could have been one more.

'It's quite a list,' Miller said. 'Makes it a horrible case, I think it's going to turn into the case of the century.'

'Right, then let's ask for an appointment with the Chief Commander and tell him what we think.'

Miller finished his drink. 'I've already done it. I fixed it up with Paul Masters... He understood and we have an appointment tomorrow. He knew the Chief Commander would want to see us.'

* * *

Although Coffin and Stella were tired when she got back, sleep and peace would not come easily. 'I'm going into the theatre tomorrow,' Stella was emphatic.

'I knew you would do.'

'There is something I want to show you now though.'

She produced from a pocket a pornographic photograph of a child.

'This was stuck in the back of my trousers when I got of the car. I don't know how it got there.' She looked at her husband. 'It must be all one case.'

After a pause, Coffin said, half to himself: 'I shall want to see everyone.'

Chapter 7

'I knew the Chief Commander would want to see everyone working on the various cases,' said Paul Masters. 'I took the liberty of calling a meeting.' This was one of the occasions when Masters' slightly pedantic way of speaking was effective.

There they all were: Superintendent Miller and Inspector Winnie Ardet sitting near each other, Sergeant Mercy Adams and Phoebe Astley facing each other across a small table.

'I think we've all thought for some time now that it was all one case,' said Phoebe. 'Felt like it, somehow.'

'You're not usually one for intuition,' said Paul.

'Growing on me,' She grinned at him. 'Comes of working with you.'

'Joe will be sorry to miss this,' said Mercy, to no one in particular. She had worked with him, and although not an easy colleague (which was not telling everything, by any means) she respected his mental powers. Mercy was back at work but looking pale. Had she come back too soon? A few more days off?

'Still not up to much?' This was Paul, never much of an admirer of Joe since they had worked together in the early days. Bit of a hypochondriac he had decided. Likewise a grabber. 'What did he say?'

'Didn't speak to him. Always hard to get through Josephine.' Joe and Josephine, thought Mercy. Is that why they married? 'His wife said he was having a bad day.'

'Having one myself,' said Paul. He stood up as Coffin came in. 'Morning, sir.'

Gus had come with his master.

'And how is Miss Pinero?' This was Jack Miller who never minded asking questions, which made him a good detective, if a difficult friend.

'Gone into the theatre, but she *is* going to see a doctor,' said Coffin with decision. 'Might go myself. It's been a bad time.' He looked around at the team, assessing their mood. 'You all know what happened to Stella and the photograph she came back with.'

'Do you think she was allowed to escape on purpose?' This was Miller again.

'Not the way she tells it.'

But does she know? thought Miller. This time he kept quiet, although he caught Phoebe's eye and guessed she was thinking the same.

'She got away, but she was dazed. She'd had a blow to the head which is why she is going to see the doctor whether she likes it or not. And I may say that she does not.' Coffin allowed himself a grin.

'She's a brave woman,' said Phoebe, who had known what it was to be in awe of Stella.

'She's an actress,' said Coffin. 'I think she's frightened enough which is why I want these two men caught.'

'If it had been a genuine black cab, that should not have been too difficult,' said Phoebe, but she said it doubtfully, her doubts accentuated when Masters said at once that it must have been stolen.

'The man could never have been a genuine, licensed cab driver.'

'That shows a nice feeling towards London cab drivers, but I agree with you. He was a phoney, a fake. He told Stella I had sent him'.

'An actor, do you think?'

There was a silence.

'Worth thinking about,' said the Chief Commander. 'Capable of putting on an act, anyway.'

Coffin knew all about theatre folk. In theory, they knew little about what had happened to Stella, but he was betting the word was already buzzing around. She had been kid-napped, she had been raped, she had been murdered. How the stories got around, he never knew, but circulate they did.

Some people looked surprised when Stella walked in, others, so she complained, looked disappointed. She herself felt less confident and cheerful than she was prepared to admit: someone out there was after her. She knew she was protected; without telling her, Coffin would have sent at least one person to guard her. She had not identified that person yet but give her time and she would. He would certainly be in and out himself on one pretext or another, and she might even encourage it. It was not going to be easy to check the comings and goings of strangers in the complex which included one large theatre, a smaller experimental theatre, and a tiny space used by schools, not to mention an even smaller one work had just begun upon. In addition there were two restaurants, one more casual and easier to walk in and out of than the other.

Stella had invented the theatre in the old, disused church of St Lukes and then she had moved with her husband into the former church tower which, to both their surprise, had converted well into a home. She took pride in the success of her theatre in the Second City of London. She was inclined to congratulate herself on the way the Second City (once the home of empty factories and derelict docks) had prospered.

She had enriched herself and the theatre, she believed, through her activities, but Mimsie Marker, that famed local figure and seller of newspapers, had warned her that success brought enemies. And Mimsie, as she pointed out, ought to know, being herself a local success story, reputed to own a Rolls (actually a Bentley, much classier, anyone could have a Rolls) and a handsome house down by the river.

Stella spent the morning reading scripts, then she had arranged to lunch with Tony Amato, a well known actor, whom she wanted to persuade to sign up for a new play. He was at the same time plain of feature and immensely attractive. To both sexes. In fact, he was practically a third sex in himself. But he never made an advance to Stella because as an employer he found it wiser to regard her as a sexual neutral. Go to bed with someone who is employing you and you can be in trouble. Besides, he feared the Chief Commander.

Stella knew all this and did not resent his behaviour.

They ate in the large dining room, at Stella's usual table in the window.

'I like what you are offering me.' Tony said as they ate.

'Oh good, I thought you would.' What was on offer was the part of a sharp-tongued but charming detective who always got his man. There was a certain humour there which all parties recognised. It would run for six weeks, not long, but the productions in St Luke's Theatre were well thought of and carefully reviewed in all the right places. In addition, a job there often led to a prestigious part elsewhere.

'I'll have to talk to Freddy, of course.'

'Of course,' Freddy Braun was his agent. 'I can't pay a lot.'

Tony grinned. 'Oh that reminds me... although I don't know why it should.' He reached in his pocket. 'As I was parking the car, a chap asked me if I knew you, when I said I did... didn't saying I was lunching with you, sounded like boasting... he asked would I give you this.' He handed over a crumpled envelope.

'Who was this man? What did he look like?'

'I didn't take much in, I was in a hurry to get to you, Stella. He had dark specs on.'

'Are you sure it's for me?' asked Stella. The envelope was crumpled but with no name on it.

'He said so. Sorry it looks like that, but I put it in my pocket and forgot it.'

'I'll open it later.'

She did open the letter when she was alone. She read:

YOU'VE GOT AWAY TWICE NOW. DON'T THINK YOU'LL GET AWAY AGAIN.

'Yes, I will,' said Stella defiantly. 'Again and again.'

Chapter 8

'What does he mean, you got away *twice*?' demanded Coffin. ' Once, yes, last night, but the other time? '

'I don't know,' said Stella.

'You must think. Try to remember.'

Stella walked to the window to look out. They were in St Luke's Tower, in the sitting room up the winding staircase. It was a room in which Stella always felt safe and happy. Gus the dog, and the cat were with them. She put out a hand to stroke the cat. 'My comfort object.' Gus pushed up to her. 'You too, dear boy.'

`She turned to her husband. 'I debated showing you the letter. I almost didn't.'

'Oh Stella, why not?'

She reached out and took his hand. 'I think I was frightened what you would do.'

'I'd always protect you, Stella.'

Sensing her distress, Gus climbed up on to her lap, the cat thought about it for a minute then followed. Stella started to laugh.

'I know.'

'I never saw the man who delivered this note, but had a sort of feeling that I knew one of the people in the car. Not the driver, I couldn't see his face, but the one that tried to get into the car. The one I pushed.'

'I wish you had told me this at once.'

'I was thinking about it, wondering if it was so and, if so, how and where.'

There was a double ring at the doorbell. Stella looked at her husband in alarm.

'It's just our dinner... I ordered it from Maxim's.'

Gus barked.

'Yes, something for you too.'

'I hope you ordered something for the cat as well.'

'Of course, I did.'

'I do love you.'

'And I love you.' More than you know, I expect, or want to think about.

'Sometimes, I'm frightened.'

'And do you think I am not?'

Stella looked at him with those large, lovely eyes, which could express so much, actresswise, of love, support, confidence, but were not doing so now. All he could read there was puzzlement and doubts.

She really thinks men are different animals, and within that species, policemen are different again.

Perhaps we are, he thought, drawing back a little. Perhaps we *are* different animals and don't know it. You might not. After all, a cat doesn't necessarily know it's not a dog.

Then he saw the young cat observing with bright green eyes, tail flicky. Oh yes, you know you are not a dog... But do you know you are a cat? That's different again, isn't it?

The cat looked at him, eyes lucid and sharp.

Yes, he decided, he knew he was a cat, and a male cat at that. Castrated too, but one who had been getting amorous with Gus, which puzzled Gus and Coffin. They must take the cat down to the vet's and do something about that.

He hurried to the door where one of Maxim's large family was carrying a tray.

'Oh thanks, it's Joe, isn't it?'

'No, I'm Jim, but we all look alike.' He grinned.

'Now let me see, are you the philosopher or the historian?' They were a clever family of six boys and one girl, but Maxim demanded that all, whatever their intellectual aspirations, worked as often as they could in the family firm, which, as he pointed out, financed their expensive educations.

'No, I'm the medical student, so I shall be in hock to my father for a while as my training takes so long.' He grinned again as he took the money from Coffin. 'Did the chap who was prowling round the theatre bar find Miss Pinero?'

'What man was that?' asked Coffin alertly.

'Didn't give a name, just asked for her, said he'd been going round looking for her and he'd lost her twice.'

'Did he indeed,' said Coffin. Police talk, he thought to himself, you don't talk like that to Stella or your friends or the cat and dog. 'What was he like?'

Jim pursed his lips. 'We were pretty busy, in fact very busy, so I didn't look hard. Tall, thin, one of those ambiguous sorts. A man probably, but really androgynous. You wonder if he even had a sex.'

Coffin thought he was lucky to have got the medical student, who was alert to nuances of sex and behaviour: he hadn't looked at the man hard, but he had thought him ambivalent and he hadn't liked him.

Jim shook his head. 'Mr Now-you-see-him, Now-you-don't.'

'Didn't *want* you to notice him, maybe?' tried Coffin.

'Oh, he wanted me to notice him all right. I could tell. I didn't like him. No reason, just one of those feelings. I wouldn't have told him where Miss Pinero was even if I had known, but I didn't.'

Coffin picked up the tray of food which he had put down 'Better start thinking of eating this.' He wasn't hungry, nor did he suppose Stella was, but life must go on.

'Sir...'

'Yes?' he turned back.

'I heard a story that another person had been stabbed... cut up. Murdered. Like the others. But a kid this time.'

'Where did you get that from?' said Coffin at once. He did not believe it.

Jim hesitated. 'I think I heard the old weirdo telling someone.'

Stuff not to tell Stella, Coffin thought, as he got away. No more bad news, please, he said to himself.

Coffin marched up the stairs to where Stella sat, carrying the tray of food which he had chosen carefully from Stella's favourite dishes. Smoked salmon, then cold roast chicken with salad and a chocolate mousse. Stella would eat the chocolate mousse under pressure, murmuring about her weight and waist, but she would enjoy it. 'You are spoiling me,' she might say, but Coffin thought she needed spoiling. And as it happened, quite by chance of course, he liked all those dishes himself.

Even policemen needed spoiling occasionally.

'You're smiling,' Stella said as he came into the room. She was sitting up, looking more composed. When she saw what he was carrying, she stood up.

'That deserves the best we can offer it. Give me ten minutes to change into something ...' she hesitated.

'More festive?'

'Something prettier anyway.' And do her hair and perhaps a little scent.

Coffin looked at her with pleasure; life was coming back into Stella, and this time she wasn't acting.

'Right,' he said. 'I'll get out the silver and set the table.'

Gus kept his eyes on the tray: he knew that smell and it meant good food. The new cat, younger, more innocent and not so used to the ways of the house, but wise, took her cue from Gus and sidled up to where he was. What he did, cat would do.

When Stella came back, she was wearing a soft apricot pink velvet gown and gold slippers. This outfit had been part of the success of 'Private Lives' in which Stella had starred. She enjoyed playing in Coward, he offered so much to an actress, and she had bought those of the costumes which suited her best. They had been made for her after all and no one else could wear them. Nor could you give them a part in the latest Pinter.

'You look like an actress,' said her husband, giving her a kiss. ' Glorious.'

Stella looked at him and laughed. 'I always know when you are lying.'

It was a verbal game in which they took much pleasure. A cut and thrust with erotic undertones appreciated and enjoyed by both parties.

She went up to him and kissed him on the cheek. 'Food, first please. After that... well, we'll see.'

It was not an occasion for champagne, Coffin had decided, although, thank God, he had Stella back, but he poured some good red wine.

When he judged the moment right, Coffin said quietly: 'We'll get the chap.'

'*Chaps*,' said Stella. 'Two of them.'

By her quickness she had let Coffin see how disturbed she was. He could not blame her.

'Yes, two men. We'll have them, Stella.'

'You think I can't face this, but I can. These men are the killers who are murdering women in the Second City. I haven't counted the deaths but I know from the way you have been behaving that there are far too many.'

'Too many,' echoed Coffin. Before his eyes he had a picture of one of the bodies he had seen on the mortuary table. They all differed slightly while having a hideous similarity. The thought that Stella might have been another of them: bloody, battered, ripped open, made him feel sick. He took some more red wine.

'You're hiding something, aren't you?' said Stella. It was a statement more than a question.

'No, of course not.' He poured her another drink.

Stella shook her head at the wine. 'I told you I could always tell when you were lying... then it was a joke, but now it's true. You are lying; you are hiding something.'

Coffin remained silent.

'Come on now, I know you're not hiding a secret mistress in New York, nor that you have helped defraud a bank of over a million because you look like such an honest police chief. Nor have you murdered anyone or shot the cat.'

The cat in question looked up alertly.

Coffin tried to laugh, but found he couldn't.

'You're trying to protect me,' said Stella, 'and that's what is frightening me.'

He could see what she meant. So he told her what he had just heard.

'I suppose I guessed. Thanks for protecting me from the bitter truth. Or trying, bless you.'

'Is that how you really feel?'

'Of course it is. ' She reached out her hand for his.

'Darling Stella.'

'Old Weirdo, yes, he sounds like my fella. I shouldn't get upset. I know I am safe with you.' She had her fingers crossed.

They were standing close together, with Gus on Coffin's feet, when the telephone rang.

'I won't answer it,' said Coffin.

Stella said sadly: 'But you must.'

He turned towards the telephone. 'I'll give it time to ring off.'

But they both knew it would not.

'It might not be for you. Shall I answer it?' Words, idle words, she thought. I'm not going to answer the call. I'm frightened and he knows I am frightened. Scared silly, but I am not going to admit it. 'No, don't answer that. I know it's for you.'

The Chief Commander would not be disturbed at home, after the sort of day he had had and been known to have, unless it was important.

Coffin picked up the telephone. 'Hello, John Coffin here.' He listened without a word. Then: 'Right, thank you, Phoebe. You want me over there?'

There was a mutter which Stella could not hear but which she could guess at. Phoebe Astley *did* want him over there, wherever there was. 'I'm not jealous of you, Phoebe, but you do pull rank on occasion. Not that I blame you: you're the detective and I'm not.' Then a wicked, irreverent thought came to her : But I have the better hairdresser.

Coffin came back, his expression hard to read.

'It's not good is it? Something bad? Another murder? It is, isn't it? No, don't answer, I know it is. We both knew it as soon as the telephone rang.'

He nodded. 'Yes, another killing.'

'One in the series?'

He hesitated. 'Probably. Seems likely. ' He would like to believe not, but he could not.

'So the old weirdo was right?'

He took his time answering. 'We can't tell yet.'

'There's something else,' said Stella. She could read his face.

'Yes,' said Coffin, sadly.

'Go on, you must tell me.'

'Not a woman but a child.'

'A child? A child may not be part of the series.' Stella was reluctant to accept it.

'The working team think so... I do too, Stella, with nothing to go on except intuition.' He hesitated before saying that he would have to go to the site and see the body. He tried for lightness. 'You'll have Gus to look after you.' In fact, he hated leaving Stella, but he would see that there was a protective presence in a police car outside St Luke's Tower. Phoebe had suggested it as a sensible precaution, which was one of the reasons for thinking this death was one of the terrible series.

'Let me come too.'

'Darling, you couldn't do anything. You would not even be allowed on the murder scene.'

'I don't want to be. I just don't want to be left behind...' She tried for a smile. 'Not even with Gus.'

* * *

Stella sat in the car, with Gus on her lap, while Coffin went behind the screened off murder site in company with Phoebe.

They were in a narrow road in Spinnergate, not far from the police HQ. It was not one of the most attractive roads in Spinnergate but it was going up in the world, with some of the old shops putting on new faces and selling pictures and books instead of herrings and pork chops. Spinnergate, richer than it had been once, now bought its food in large supermarkets, or got on the train and went to Harrods or Fortnum and Masons. Coffin saw that one shop was renting hats, which surprised him and made him realise what a sheltered life he led, they were beautiful hats too. Beyond was an area hidden behind a white tentlike affair inside which, he knew, was the body. A uniformed constable stood on guard. At the kerb he recognised the pathologist's car.

'Got there before me,' he thought with some guilt. On the other hand he knew that several of the investigating officers whom he had chosen were there already.

'You brought Stella with you,' said Phoebe, who looked untidy, tired and harassed.

'She didn't want to be left behind.'

'Can't blame her. You won't like what you are about to see,' said Phoebe as she led him forward. 'The body was found about an hour and a half ago by a boy delivering papers.'

'You got this set up quickly.' She was efficient, was Phoebe, one of the reasons for her promotion. She would probably go higher, too.

Phoebe shrugged. 'Had to. We mind about these killings. Especially this one. You'll see why.' She led him forward. 'The pathologist says he was killed about four hours earlier.'

'Late afternoon then,' said Coffin.

Inside the covered area, he nodded to the two Scene of Crime officers, then stared down at the small, bloody figure.

'He's very young.'

'Not as young as he looks. Just small boned. Partly a racial inheritance. We know his name, he had a card in his pocket: Charlie Fisher... anyway, one of the officers on duty, DC Edith Dinks recognised him, she knows his mother. You may too or Stella may, she came from Hong Kong to work here and got a job in the wardrobe rooms in St Luke's Theatre.'

'I don't know her.'

'The kid worked in the theatre too, an apprentice stage hand: Charlie Chan was his nickname.'

'You've done a lot in a very short time. Good. How was he killed? Strangled wasn't he?'

'Yes, the first use of a tie round the throat... then cut up afterwards.'

Coffin nodded, 'Was he dead when he was cut?'

'Dr Jerome... you saw him?'

'He was just leaving as I arrived. We didn't speak.'

'He says he can tell us more once he gets the body on the table in the mortuary. He thinks he was dead before the knife went in.'

'Poor little soul..' He knelt down and lifted the right hand. Then he stood up shaking his head. 'Makes me sick. ' He moved away. Behind him he heard Phoebe say, as if to herself: 'There's something iffy about this case The way the bodies are laid out.'

'You don't usually talk like that,' said the young DC who was taking notes.

'I don't usually feel like it.'

Stella was out of the car when Coffin returned, standing on the kerb, nursing the dog.

'Well?' she said.

He knew what the query meant: how was he killed, was he badly cut up, and who was he?

He answered the last bit first because he would have to come across with the identity but might get away without talking about what had been done to him.

'A lad, half Chinese, called Charlie Fisher. You might know him, he worked in the theatre. So did his mother.'

'Charlie Chan? Little Charlie, of course I knew him. Does his mother know?'

'I expect she does by now.' He put his arm round her and drew her to the car. 'Come on, let's get off. I've done all I can for the moment.'

Stella resisted. 'I want to see him.'

'No. Can't be done.' There was no way he was going to let Stella see the boy's body. 'Sorry, love.'

She stood there without moving. 'Once again there's more than you are saying. It's worse. What was done to him?

Gus growled softly.

'Come on, let's get home.'

'Tell me, ' commanded Stella.

Coffin took a deep breath. 'His hands were cut.'

'How?'

Suddenly Coffin could not keep it back. 'His fingers were completely cut off.'

Phoebe had appeared outside the white tent. She saw the Chief Commander put his arms round his wife and draw her into the car.

Phoebe wished she had someone to put their arms around her. She knew by now she was to work on the serial killings as part of the investigation. 'Concentrate there', the Chief Commander had told her himself.

Did he mean it was more her style or that she was getting dangerously obsessed with the paedophile business?

She would find it hard to forget Charlie.

Chapter 9

An early mentor of John Coffin had said to him: Always keep ahead of the game. On the whole he had tried, and often succeeded in this, but at the moment he felt he was way behind. He did not even know the name of the game let alone the rules to play by.

Better not to let Stella know this. She was a great guesser, though.

'You think that this killer will never be caught. It frightens you. Your first failure.'

'I've had plenty of others,' he observed mildly.

He was thinking of the killer who had shot two young men and dropped their bodies in the river Thames on the south side. Almost certainly a homophobic killing, but the murderer had never been caught. There was the person who dropped poison into a dish of icecream in a stall outside Fenshone Park behind the tube station - no one actually died but a score of children had a bad time. Then there was the man who almost certainly killed two wives before topping himself. You couldn't call that a success. And they were only the ones he knew about, the worse ones are those that he never knew about at all.

'I won't name them,' he said, 'but you probably could do it. You lived with me through them.'

'Those were professional failures,' observed Stella. ' You didn't mind them in a really *personal* way. '

'I wish you hadn't said that.'

'This murderer knows us. Knows you, knows me. That is why you are worried. I think it is true. '

Coffin nodded. 'OK, yes, he does feel close. Man or woman. I don't rule out a woman.'

He had felt a feminine element.

'I don't like the feel of it.'

'You don't usually talk like that,' Stella remarked.

'Phoebe feels the same way.'

The professional mind, thought Stella.

The body of the girl in Pepper Alley had, as yet, no name.

'It's Peppard Alley really,' said Inspector Winnie Ardet, the purist. She, with the others, knew what had happened to Stella and the news of Charlie's body and wondered where it fitted in. At least Stella had not been attacked in Peppard Alley, she thought with relief.

'Can't make much difference to the death.'

'Might make some difference to finding out who killed her, perhaps.'

Superindenent Miller, Winnie Ardet, Phoebe Astley and the other officers involved on the cases were all in the smaller briefing room in the central police station which all disliked from unhappy memories of the past but which remained one of the few rooms for general use, rank or case unheeded. It was a heavily masculine room with leather furniture and a big table that looked as though it had been used to dance on in boots. (As indeed it had been, to celebrate the last successful case in which Miller and Ardet had been involved. They had not done the dancing but they had clapped along with the best.) It was also a room in which you could be reasonably safe from an entrance by the Chief Commander. He knew what went on there, having an excellent private intelligence service, but he approved rather than felt alarmed. This was their second meeting in as many days.

'Let's put the victims in place,' said the methodical Superintendent Miller. 'We can't get far till we do that. Where each lived and worked matters. To us if not to the killers.'

'You think there was more than one murderer?' asked Winnie. 'You could be right.'

'I was just speculating. Let's get on,' he said irritably.

Amy Buckly; Spinnergate, lived and worked there. School teacher.

Mary Rice; Spinnergate, worked in central London. Computer expert.

Phillida Jessup. Lived in Spinnergate. Student.

Angela Dover. Lived across the river in Greenwich. Worked in Spinnergate; office worker. Former secretary to Coffin.

'All concentrated on Spinnergate,' said Miller. 'We don't know yet about the latest victim, but I guess that she too will turn out to live or work in Spinnergate.'

'Can we take it then that the killer also works and or lives in Spinnergate?'

'It might be unwise to assume too much,' said the cautious Inspector Ardet. 'But he or she certainly knows the district. Whether that's any help or otherwise to us we shall find out.'

'We must establish the identity of the body in Peppard Alley, ' said Phoebe Astley. She had prepared herself carefully for this meeting, anxious to answer any question adequately. She knew she was facing a wide awake and sceptical audience in the police officers. 'Do your best, Phoebe,' the Chief Commander had said. 'I think everything could explode if we don't make some progress on bringing in the criminal.'

'I have made a little way forward,' said Les Henderson, Sergeant, who had hitherto kept quiet. He found the rest of this group intimidating so he was reluctant to speak unless he had something definite to say. This trait was to endear him greatly to the rest of the team while alarming them somewhat at the same time. 'Les will go straight to the top,' was their conviction even if unexpressed.

'They were not exactly unknown to the police, these ladies... No nothing criminous, just that each lady within the last twelve months has made complaints about the police.' He added. 'They didn't get lucky. Got nothing back.'

'Robbed, were they?' Miller was quick.

'Each and every one,' said Les Henderson. 'Not for the same amounts. Varied.'

'Of course, I knew that Phillida had been robbed,' said

Winnie Ardet with some irritation. 'Robbed and the police were no good at all. I was one of the investigating team and know that we failed.'

'Oh go on,' said Miller. 'They tried.'

'If you're the victim and you lose your grandmother's pearl and diamond earrings that you have just inherited then trying is not enough: you want them back.' Winnie had got the force of Phillida's tongue so she knew how the victim felt.

'Not the only victim. Amy Buckley had her car stolen... she did get it back but somewhat battered.'

There was a list which silently, all members studied. It might help them, it might not.

Mary Rice, lost her mongrel dog. Never got it back. Probably in Aberdeen by now. Aged 22, lived alone, a flat in a large block by the tube station .

Angela Dover. Aged 39. She had a small house in the middle of Greenwich, overlooking the Thames. She was attacked and robbed (raped, she hinted, but no one believed this and such medical inspection as she submitted to did not bear it out), she named her attacker but it was hard to prove him guilty. Just one of those tricky cases from which no one emerges with credit. Angela had certainly hurled accusations around, even attacking the police. No one believed her, but dirt sticks. Angela stayed around in the Second City writing indignant letters to the local press and asking for an interview, repeatedly denied, on the television news from City Central. Of course now Angela had achieved the ultimate publicity stroke by being murdered.

The last victim who had not been named at first had now only just been identified. The report came in to the meeting: she was said to be Charlotte, more commonly known as Lotty, Brister. Age unconfirmed but probably near retirement. Miss Brister was the owner of a shop in Spinnergate but like another victim she too lived across the river in Greenwich, near the Park. She had just put her shop up for sale, likewise her house in Greenwich, saying she was moving to the seaside to be near her sister. All this was very new information and except for the sale of the shop, which was advertised, might not be true. All needed double-checking as Superintendent Miller pointed out.

'A wide age range,' said Miller. 'I wonder if that means anything?' He was looking for help all round and knew it.

'Nothing except they were out and around at a convenient time when the killer wanted to work.' This was from Winnie Ardet.

'So nothing personal, we think? Just an accidental choice?'

'No, that can't be,' said Phoebe who had kept as quiet as she could. 'I think the killer knew them or something about them. The Chief Commander thinks so too... he thinks he is on the list.'

'I think that too,' said Les Henderson, surprising himself. His voice had popped out louder than he had meant. 'He knew them. Even tracked them down, maybe.'

'Except for the tracking down,' said Winnie slowly, 'I am coming round to that view.' What the Chief Commander thought she was willing to think too. Added to which she had learnt to take Phoebe Astley's judgement as reliable, as well as admiring Phoebe's long-legged athletic look. Winnie was heavy boned and solid but she had beautiful fair hair which she kept well cut and groomed.

'I hope we are looking after the Chief Commander,' said Les. 'We'd miss him all right. And Miss Pinero, her ladyship.' He admired Stella, just as he also admired Winnie. On the short side himself and with big hands, but he liked to think with a bigger than average brain, he knew he was no beauty.

'You needn't worry about the boss,' said Phoebe shortly. 'He's been through this sort of thing before. We are keeping an eye on him, and also on Stella after her attack.'

Word of which had been going round the Second City Force with speed.

'So we shall be watching for her.'

'I've heard that she actually saw the man who might be our serial killer,' said Henderson.

'Yes, ' agreed Phoebe. 'All two of him.'

'What?'

'In her case, two men were involved.'

'How did she get away?'

Phoebe had wondered about this herself. 'Luck,' she said shortly.

'She can be very helpful to us in finding and identifying the killer,' said Miller.'

'Maybe,' said Phoebe. 'One of the men was masked, the other, the driver of the car, which *was* stolen by the way, she only saw briefly and is sure his face was made up. She could smell make-up. She is a performer, remember, and would know.'

The car had been taken from outside Waterloo station, reported as stolen by the owner and identified when dumped outside a police station on the Greenwich to Deptford Road.

'Didn't know there was one,' observed Les.

'Oh just off it.'

'Yes, there is a station there. He's local, this killer, has to be,' Les again. 'And what about that remark of hunting in pairs? Sinister and we shouldn't forget it.'

'May not mean anything,' said someone.

'Or the double-headed man,' joked someone else, causing Les to grind his teeth in irritation.

'You don't have to live locally to get local knowledge,' said Miller. 'He could walk around, prospect, work things out. I've done it myself.'

For a deliriously happy moment, Les pictured Miller as a criminal, a murderer even, then he pushed the thought away.

'He has some local links, this killer,' said Phoebe firmly. 'We mustn't disagree too much here, we must come to a common judgement if we are to get anywhere.'

'I think disagreement counts,' said Les. 'Lets things out of the bag.'

Miller went to the door, then came back with a tray laden with cups. 'Tea, I ordered it. Thought we'd need something. There is coffee for those who prefer. I reckon tea clears the brain better.'

Most of them took tea because the coffee was so poor. The tea tasted of something, as Les had said once, whereas the coffee was just dark coloured water. 'Sometimes not even hot,' Les had added. 'Although I remember one case where the chill of the coffee helped me... it was in Shillingford. Remember that case, do you?'

'Shut up, Les,' said Winnie. 'You're rambling.'

'No, only trying to help one and all clear their minds,' said Les, not at all hurt, and who knew exactly what he was doing, perhaps not exactly clearing the mind as much as stopping the slight altercations that were breaking out, as they always did at such meetings. He was not exactly a man of peace but he liked to get on with the job, and arguing did not help.

'What we have to talk about now,' said Phoebe firmly, feeling she was the voice of the Chief Commander, 'is how we catch this serial killer.'

'By working bloody hard,' said Les.

Phoebe laughed. 'I know you are a hard worker, Les. But intelligence and thought comes into it too. I can trust you there.'

'Can we be sure that the same killer is at work with all the victims?' Les asked.

There was a mutter from his colleagues.

'Right. On the whole we think so. Frankly, I can't believe that we have two different serial killers working at the same time in the Second City. Not saying it is impossible, but not *likely*. So we have one killer.'

'Two killers according to Stella.' This was Miller.

'I accept that: two men working together. Possibly not all the time.' Phoebe spoke quietly.

'If once, then the second man is always there in the

background.' This was Les. 'Whatever that background is. Not sure if I know at this moment.'

'It should be easier to locate two men than just one,' said Winnie. 'or am I being over-hopeful?'

'Hopeful,' said a voice from the door. The Chief Commander had arrived. He had not been expected, except perhaps by Phoebe. She knew that Stella had been persuading him to find out exactly what was being said and done.

'No one tells me anything,' she had complained to Phoebe, 'and I am a victim: I want to know.'

'There may not be much to tell,' Phoebe had said, although she knew that the Chief Commander was well able to keep what secrets he chose.

'I think I'll make him retire. He's got his knighthood, although as far as I can see he rarely uses it. '

'Could you make him retire?'

'No,' said Stella, without hesitation.

Phoebe looked at her quizzically.

'No,' said Stella, 'he couldn't make me retire either. In fact, I am having a particularly successful run.'

So Phoebe was not surprised to see the Chief Commander come into the room. 'Stella's putting on the heat,' he had said to her and Paul Masters only an hour or two ago. 'Can't blame her.'

'Any coffee for me?' he asked, advancing towards the tray.

Superintendent Miller poured him a cup. 'Hope it's hot enough.'

It wasn't hot but Coffin drank it. Nor was it strong. So not a good cup of coffee but he didn't drink it with that in mind, it was more a social gesture. The tea was probably more reliable but bound to be dark and stewed by now.

'How are things?' he asked, putting his cup down.

'We're talking everything through,' said Miller. 'I expect you know how it goes, sir, at this time in this sort of case.'

'We haven't had a serial murder for some time, I'm glad to admit,' Coffin answered.

Phoebe could see that he had come with a message.

'The local television news programme asked to interview us about these murders. They wanted Stella as well, in fact I am sure it was Stella they really wanted. You know "famous actress talks to us about the attack on her". Stella didn't want to do it, she doesn't want to talk about what happened except in what you might call an "official kind of way" - in other words except to you lot, you can ask her what you like and if she can help, she will. But the interview idea itself is valuable and so I suggested two of you.'

Phoebe looked thoughtful. She could see what was coming her way.

'So I suggested you, Phoebe, and Jack Miller.'

Winnie Ardet was disappointed: she would have enjoyed it, but she recognised that Phoebe Astley had the greater status.

Phoebe and Superintendent Miller looked at each other. They were not friends but they knew how to behave. If they had to do an interview together, then so be it.

'I think Winnie would be better at this interview than me, sir,' said Phoebe. 'I'm not bad on the radio, but I never do well on TV. I suggest Winnie takes my place, she always comes across as very natural.'

Winnie looked gratified, although well aware that she had never been on television and if she had then it was very doubtful Phoebe would have seen her.

'I don't mind doing it,' she said. 'If the Superintendent agrees.'

Miller nodded, he would prefer Winnie.

'See my secretary, she'll give you the details.' Coffin walked to the table on which were spread notes about the cases. 'A bit more information has just come in about the latest victim: Lotty Brister. She was seen getting into a car and going off with the man who may have been her killer.'

'That's the only sighting we've had,' said Ted.

'So far,' said the Chief Commander. 'It would be very

helpful to have some others. Stella has put her bit in, of course, but it hasn't helped much yet. May do in time. In these affairs it is a matter of adding one fact to another till we get a shape, a picture.`

'So he uses a taxi? Is that the suggestion? '

'Could be,' said Coffin who was having one of those moments when his mind cleared and he seemed to see everything hard and bright.

'You sound doubtful.'

'If I was a serial killer, hoping to get away with it, then I wouldn't always use the same technique.'

'A taxi might be a good idea,' said Winnie,' but you would have to own the taxi, not borrow it or hire it, too risky.'

'Do you mean the killer is a taxi driver?' The suggestion was made again by someone at the back of the room.

For some reason this silenced discussion.

'I thought you were going to tell us something else, sir,' said Phoebe Astley.

'Yes, the last victim called herself Lotty Brister, that name meant something to me, so I got Paul Masters to do some digging. He didn't have to look far: it was a name she had started to use after she came out of prison.'

The room came to attention.

'Yes, she'd been inside for a particularly nasty murder. A new name for a new life seemed a good idea, I suppose.'

'I remember the case now,' said Inspector Winnie Ardet.'Yes, it was nasty, a child, wasn't it? She claimed it was an accident but not many people believed it. There was a bit of sympathy, she was quite young herself.'

'Well, she was older when she was killed,' said Coffin. 'She served her sentence.' He too remembered the case, not one of his, but some cases you recall. Mary James, she was then, (and even that did not sound like a real name so perhaps she was inventive there too) he didn't know where the name under which she died came from. No doubt they would find out as the investigation went on.

'Do you think her killer knew her for what she was?' Jack Miller wanted to know. 'An ex con?'

'Be interesting, wouldn't it?' Les Henderson said. He had been silent for some time, but thoughtful. He was one of the cleverest of the present team, one whom Coffin had marked down as a man likely to go right to the top. Coffin looked at him now in his baggy jeans and turtleneck sweaters and thought Well, I suppose he knows how to dress the part, only what part?

Coffin was grooming Les for a rapid rise upwards, but should that include clothes? But perhaps Les had got it right, times had changed. He would have to consult Stella, she would know, you could trust Stella's judgement on matters of dress. His own clothes were, he knew, ordinary. But for him that was right, it was safer for him to look unnoticeable. Good but not memorable, that was the style of his suits. Stella had taken one look at his clothes after they came together again after years apart, and sent him to Mr Herries, the tailor who made suits for the best productions in town.

'Boss figure but not flashy,' she had ordered.

Apparently Mr Herries knew what she meant because he measured Coffin up and delivered a wardrobe of some six suits whose price alarmed Coffin but which came as a present from Stella. There must have been something in Mr Herries' eye and cut because with in a few months Coffin was offered and accepted the position of Chief Commander of the Police in the Second City. He was still wearing the suits. He intended to be still wearing them when he retired. Stella, of course, would never retire, she would be performing into any new millennium, and as long as she was there, working in the theatre, he would be close by.

He looked towards Miller. 'What about the post mortem reports, any help there?'

Miller nodded. As senior detective, all these reports were coming to him first. 'I'm collating them all, then I'll pass them on with my comments. A couple of doctors are working on the bodies. They do what's necessary and let me know. But each victim was killed in the same way: manual strangulation and the later ones were then cut up with a sharp knife, rape but no semen. Forensics are still at work, of course. I'm hoping to get something there. But nothing helpful so far.' He yawned. One way and another he hadn't got much sleep lately, he was getting too tired to think. He saw the Chief Commander looking at him with what might have been sympathy and might not. 'Sorry, sir.' He began to sneeze, a cascade of sneeezes. 'Sorry,' he muttered,' an allergy, I think.'

'How's Lady Coffin?... Miss Pinero,' said Les Henderson hastily. Partly because he could see Miller was embarrassed but more because he wanted to know. Everyone liked Stella.

'Behaving well, too well, really, I wish she'd talk about it a bit more. She's told all she can that helps.' He frowned. 'I am worried about her safety.'

'We are looking after her, sir, I promise you.'

Coffin smiled at Les. 'I know. And I am keeping an eye on her too, don't worry.'

'None of us will rest till we've caught this chap. He's a clever bugger, but he'll make a mistake... and then we'll have him.'

Coffin hoped his young friend was right. He walked back to his office to find a telephone call from Stella waiting for him.

'You ought to be resting.'

'I am resting. Well, in a way. There's something that I wanted to tell you. '

He could tell by her voice that she was enjoying herself. His own spirits lightened. 'Come on, what's it all about?'

'First, I don't think I was in any danger, they wanted to frighten me, or you, but not actually to harm. They wanted to make an impression.'

'They did that all right.' He at least took the 'hunting in pairs' seriously.

'But if I hadn't escaped, then I guess they would have seen that I did.'

'If you say so.'

'So, they *wanted* me to escape.'

'Did they happen to explain why?' Coffin was sceptical.

'No, but they were acting. I could tell. Made-up, dressed up. Wigged up and acting.' She sounded triumphant.

'You're the expert,' said Coffin reluctantly. 'If you say they were acting, then they were.'

'Yes, you have to admit that I know what I am talking about.' Stella was not laughing. 'I don't know *why* the act was put on but I knew it for what it was. But I'm not sure that they wanted me to know they were acting. '

'So they didn't want you to know them in their real persona? Is that what you are saying?'

'I'm not sure what I'm saying. You're the detective. I'm just giving you information, you work out what it means.'

Stella sounded very confident and almost gay. But she was an actress as Coffin reminded himself. As far as he was concerned the idea of the killer being an actor did not appeal, but he would pass it on to Phoebe and tell her to see it did the rounds.

Phoebe took what he had to say calmly.

'Reckon she was in a state to make a judgement?'

'On that sort of topic, yes. She's a pro', don't forget'. She didn't say a good actor, just acting.'

'Too much to hope she might recognise him?'

'Yes,' said Coffin. 'What do you want... Stella to solve the case?'

'Wouldn't mind,' said Phoebe. 'It'd give us all a good laugh.'

Especially Stella, thought Coffin.

'Leave it with us, sir,' said Phoebe, 'each investigating team will be working on it.' Although I don't know exactly what and how, she thought, something will give somewhere.

She did what she thought Coffin intended she should do

by telephoning round the group to tell them what Stella had to say.

On drinking a cup of strong canteen coffee while she thought it over, surprisingly she found herself valuing Stella's contribution. But this was because she had come to have a high opinion of Stella Pinero.

Tacitly she admitted to herself that when she first came to the Second City to work under the Chief Commander she, Phoebe, had been jealous of Stella.

There had been a short episode between Phoebe and John Coffin when they both worked on a case together in Birmingham. Phoebe remembered it with more intensity than the Chief Commander who, as she knew now, had just met Stella Pinero again.

'And who am I to compete with Stella?' she had asked herself more than once. Later, she had accepted the Chief Commander's offer of an important promotion to work in the Second City. It was a good job, she wanted it. One or two passing loves had come into her life, at least one remaining as a good friend, but during that time she had certainly not liked Stella.

But now, she found herself both admiring and respecting the other woman. So she passed on to the heads of each investigating team Stella's judgement that the men who attacked her were acting.

She found she quite enjoyed doing it, meeting with a mixture of incredulity and belief.

'Yes, I know how you feel, I felt the same at first, but I trust Stella's professional eye. She didn't say they were good performers, just that they were performing. Putting on an act.'

'Are we allowed to talk to her?' Les Henderson enquined.

'No, that's why I've been told. I'm the go between.' Phoebe added: 'Her initial statement was made to Paul Masters... with the Chief Commander in charge.'

'Stella has to be protected.'

'Of course, only not as much as he thinks, she's a tough lady.'

'If the killers - there do now seem to be two which we didn't know - think that Stella can identify them, they will be very keen to get her.'

'It's stranger than that though, she thinks they wanted to threaten her then let her go.'

Les thought about it. Phoebe always enjoyed it when he thought about things, she found him very attractive then. Dangerous but true.

'That means,' said Les, 'that the disguise was for her only, and not used any other time. So that she would think of them like that but they don't look like that.'

'When doing the other murders.'

'This is getting complicated.'

'It's always been that,' said Phoebe.

Phoebe and Les had a drink together; her invitation, his keen acceptance.

'How d'you like working for his lordship?' he asked over his vodka and lemon.

'It's fine,' said Phoebe, somewhat surprised at the directness of the question. 'He's a decent sort. Very decent. I've known him a long time.' She raised an eyebrow. 'Since you are asking, what about you?'

'He's bloody attractive,' said Les gloomily. 'That's always difficult for a man to take on board. Easier for a woman.'

Do you think so? said Phoebe to herself. Different, but not easier.

'He's got Stella,' she said aloud.

'She is a beauty and a lovely actress. And she never seems to change.'

Phoebe refrained from pointing out that Stella had access to, and used, the best possible professional help with her appearance. It was her job, after all.

'Perhaps we ought to get Stella to tour the streets to see if she recognises her attackers.'

'I expect she'd be game,' said Phoebe who knew how Stella reacted, 'but the Chief Commander would shoot the idea down in flames.'

'So he would. Couldn't blame him.'

He finished the drink which Phoebe had given him and accepted another.

'Oh well, may be luck will be on our side.'

Luck was. If you could call it luck. It depended which side of the game you stood.

The murderer (not that he called himself that, the "publicist for crime" was a title he might have used, if he believed in labels) was the nameless one. And he thought the luck was his.

He was sure that he had left his victims voiceless so that they could neither describe him nor name him.

Except for Miss Pinero, a little joke there, but he didn't think she would have much of value to tell the Chief Commander.

As for the rest: voiceless. So he thought.

Phoebe and Les were ending their meal in the new eating place near the police headquarters where the food was very tasty and the service both friendly and quick. 'And you don't often get both,' Les had said.

The mobile rang in Phoebe's bag. She fished it out. 'Oh Winnie...' She looked at Les. 'It's Winnie Ardet.' She listened to Winnie talking rapidly. 'Right, right, thanks for telling me. I think I'd like to see her.'

'If it's anything good that I can have then I want to come too. ' He drained his wine. 'I'm coming too then, love.' But he said it to himself.

Chapter 10

Everyone had their secrets.

'Dearest Stella,' said Coffin. He said it hopefully and sadly. Experience had told him that Stella could be immovable when she had made up her mind. 'You ought to take things quietly.'

' No, I'm better working.'

'It was a bad thing that happened to you. I wish I could have protected you from it.' I think it happened because you are my wife. He didn't say this aloud.

'Well, you are protecting me now, don't think I haven't noticed... there's always a figure not too far away from me. Man, sometimes a woman. Looked like a kid once, but I expect she was older than she looked.'

'You're too clever by half, Stella.' I've got you protected, and you need it. I do not know why but all these deaths are connected to you. Again, he did not say this aloud, but it was what he was coming to believe. A detective of long experience comes to trust his own instincts, he breathes it in, through his nostrils and down his throat, a miasma that gets into his brain.

But why Stella? Perhaps it's me, after all... But no, it was Stella. He knew it.

Just not why.

'Yes, I want you looked after. Somehow it is aimed at you. I've known it ever since that painted up pretend woman was sent into our house. Our home.'

Did he say that aloud? He could hear Stella making noises of denial down the telephone line, so he must have said something.

'Marvellous publicity if we could go public with it,' said Stella hopefully. She felt she ought to be awarded something out of what had happened to her. In her mind, bums on seats and sympathetic applause for her latest show would just do it. 'We can't,' Coffin replied in a stern voice. 'I don't want the perp to think I can read him at all.' If indeed he was doing. A thought came to him. 'Now don't go behind my back on this.'

'As if I would.'

'I don't want to see your lovely face and your "own story" splashed all over the tabloids.'

Stella laughed. She would do it if she could get away with it. Had she been threatened, had she been frightened? Yes to both questions, but she wanted to be the one who fought back.

'They're not going to get me.'

'I hope you're right.'

'I would like to think I could pick them out in a crowd, but I don't know. I am sure neither normally looked that way.' Would anyone if they could help it, she asked herself. In her profession you knew how to put yourself over.

'Actors?' Coffin enquired once more.

'Could be. Certainly acting then. From a circus, maybe.' Stella laughed. 'Especially the tall thin one, a bit of a giraffe... And don't think I don't know that you've let me go on talking so you can check where I am and what I am doing on one of those other machines you've got working for you. I hope that nice young woman has reported well on me... unless she's gone off duty, of course.' Stella, who had her own spies, knew that she had not.

'She says you are sitting with a pile of scripts in front of you and having your hair dressed.'

'Yes,' agreed Stella. 'That fracas I was in didn't half upset my hair.' She turned to the girl who was moving a comb gently over her head. 'Keep it smooth, dear, that's my style.'

The girl smiled. 'I know, Miss Pinero, you've got lovely hair, it's a pleasure to do it.'

'Thank you, Miranda, just a spray now, and it will do. Thank you.'

She smiled at the young policewoman who was drinking a cup of coffee opposite her. 'You still there, John? See you later, let's eat together tonight. You can do the cooking... Oh, I have the dog with me, just in case you wondered.'

As to the cat who knew?

'It's as well to keep your husband wondering about you, ' Stella advised the young detective after she hung up. 'The odd secret or two. Useful, bear it in mind.'

'Does the husband have secrets too?' the young detective grinned. 'Not the Chief Commander, of course, other husbands. Do they have secrets?'

'You're the copper,' said Stella. 'You ought to know.'

Stella may have had her secrets but Coffin had his too.

It was not by chance that he had kept Stella talking, he wanted to make sure that she was still safely occupied at the theatre in her office or at the hairdressers, when he went off to hear what Inspector Winnie Ardet had to say. Phoebe Astley had given him the outline, but he wanted to no must, talk to Inspector Ardet and her informant himself.

In the normal way, he would have summoned Inspector Ardet to his office and told her to bring her informant with her, but now he wanted to be the one in action. He felt the need to be on the move.

So Stella had the dog with her, but it might be wise to feed the cat in case he was detained long. He telephoned Phoebe Astley who had been waiting for his call.

'Meet me at St Luke's. Then drive with me to where Inspector Ardet is. I take it she's with the woman?'

'Yes, she felt it was safer to stay with her.'

'Hysterical, is she?'

'Inclined to be, yes. Glad you are coming, sir, because we all feel it will be better if you get it straight from her.'

Coffin drove to St Luke's. He went straight to the tower but looked hard at the old church now subsumed into the theatre complex. Somewhere in there was Stella.

He let himself into the tower, realising with new force how

he would have felt if Stella had not escaped and come home. He could feel the imagined pain like a heavy stone inside him.

He fed the cat who was asleep in his basket in the kitchen, waking him up with a stroking hand and a dish of fish. 'Have to give you a name soon.'

The cat yawned. A name? Was it eatable?

The young cat was aware of the presence of the old cat's ghost - some might call it the smell, so clear to him but as nothing to human noses. It told him a lot - that the cat had lived a happy life. It told him, more importantly, that he had found a good home. He would stay.

To underline this, he purred at Coffin, bending his head over the offered food. He wasn't that fond of fish, preferring rabbit or the captured mouse but he would oblige.

Chief Inspector Astley was waiting patiently in her car. She got out when she saw John Coffin advancing towards her. 'I'm still fond of you, you bastard,' she said inside herself, ' but you're better off with Stella. It always was Stella, anyway, wasn't it? And anyone with a mother like yours who kept on the move the way she did, lying all the time as far as I can see, was bound to make a tricky husband. Except, of course to someone like Stella, not perhaps intellectually his master but well in control aesthetically and emotionally. Somewhat like that cat of his, really.'

Aloud, she said: 'I'll drive, sir, I know the way and you may not.'

John Coffin, unaware that he was being summed up and found, to a degree, wanting, nodded. 'Accepted gratefully.'

'I told Winnie to expect us both. ' Didn't want her to panic when she saw the Chief Commander walking in.

Phoebe drove competently through the back streets of the Second City. She was not a native born Second Citizen and returned regularly to Birmingham to see her married sister and her nephews and nieces. It seemed a city in which to be happy so she always left rapidly in case she found herself joining the married tribe. You could be miserable in the Second City but at least you could be free.

Without knowing it, Phoebe and the cat also had something in common.

'You gave that motorbike a near shave,' observed Coffin mildly.

'Sorry... I was thinking.'

'Always dangerous. I was thinking myself. About Stella. I wonder if I ought to ask her to go to New York for a bit.'

'You think she'd be safer there? '

Phoebe was turning left into Merrydrew Road where Inspector Ardet's car could already be seen parked outside a semi-detached house halfway down the road. Phoebe grunted. Winnie had not left her much room to park, but she managed it. There was Winnie at the door waiting for them and behind her was the owner of the house .

'She looks nervous,' thought Phoebe as she walked up the garden path behind Coffin. Then she recognised the woman and realised she was right to be nervous.

Coffin held out his hand. 'It's Mrs Thistle, isn't it?' So you're out, he was thinking. Term of imprisonment over, shortened for good behaviour.

Mrs Thistle had run the neatest trio of brothels in the Second City, a city hardly in need of sexual outlets what with various clubs and nightspots catering for most tastes. But Mrs Thistle had targeted the crews of the ships that sidled up the river still and had done good business.

Coffin had been particularly active in seeing she was closed down.

'Mrs *Owner*, Angie Owner,' said Angie, uneasily, 'I've married again.'

'Oh,' Coffin looked around him.

'He 's away, he travels a lot,' said Mrs Owner, still uneasy.

Probably would be myself, thought Coffin if I was married to you, Angie.

By this time they were in the house. It was neat, clean, and very tidy. The furniture was good. Mrs Owner had obviously hung on to some of her ill-gotten money.

'So you know something about these serial killings that you want to tell us,' said Coffin bluntly.

'Mrs Owner has already told me. I thought she ought to tell you.' Inspector Ardet broke in. 'CI Astley agreed with me. Mrs Owner found one of the victims. The first one, Amy Buckly. The corner of Battle Street. Amy was still alive, barely, but she was. And she spoke."

Coffin felt cold inside. At the same time, hot with anger, which made it a nasty mixture. 'Why was this not reported at the time? I take it Mrs Owner did not speak out?'

Winnie looked at Mrs Owner who lowered her head as she said: 'I didn't tell anyone then that I had found Amy, I just rang the police and said there was a dead woman at the corner of Battle Street... I didn't say who I was.'

She looked defensively at the Chief Commander.

'Well, you know why.'

Winnie Ardet, still defensive, said: 'You can see why, sir. She'd had a bad time.'

Earned, Coffin thought, and enjoyed the earnings, the bad time came afterwards .

'I thought I'd just keep quiet and stay out of things... I mean that sort of thing.'

'Killings, you mean? Bloody murder of innocent women?' Was that really his voice, uttering such self-righteous, sanctimonious sludge that had never yet brought a killer home? 'So what made you change your mind? You are here now and claiming to have something valuable to say.' He looked at Inspector Ardet.

'She really has,' said Winnie.

'Come on then, spit it out. Don't waste my time.'

'I was frightened... she spoke and I heard what she said. I thought the killer would come after me if he knew.'

The Chief Commander looked at Winnie Ardet.

'I said we'd protect her,' said Winnie simply.

Winnie was a good officer and no fool. She might have chummed up with Mrs Owner, they'd probably been at school together, but she'd want something positive and real out of her.

And so do I. The thought was like a command. For Stella. He knew without a word being said that both Winnie and Phoebe also thought that Stella was concerned.

'So what happened?'

'She couldn't speak properly, hardly at all, because of her throat... I was surprised to hear anything, but I did. She said "He told me that I was only a stand-in."... then she said "No Star".... she stopped talking then... I suppose that was when she died.'

Stand-in... Star.

She said the words again, her voice still puzzled. 'I don't know if it's any help to know this but Winnie said I should tell you.'

'Yes,' said Coffin slowly. 'Thank you.'

They stood outside, Coffin, Phoebe and Winnie Ardet facing each other for a moment in silence. He looked backwards over his shoulder at the house where he could see Mrs Owner looking out of the window.

'Will she be all right?'

Winnie Ardet nodded. 'I'll see she is, sir.'

'She's a friend?'

'In a way, sir. I've known her since I could walk... earlier, really, our mothers knew each other. My mum asked me to keep looking after her... I went on knowing her even when...' She hesitated.

'I know what you don't want to say. I helped put her away. It must have been difficult for you.'

'It was,' said Winnie with feeling.

Coffin and Phoebe Astley walked towards their car, with Winnie trailing.

'Is there a Mr Owner? Or is that an invention?'

'No, there is, I met him once but he does travel a lot.'

'Can we trust what she says?'

'Oh yes, she'd tell the truth to me.'

'And what made her come out with it now?'

There was a pause. 'You may find this hard to believe, sir but she liked women, despite her business. And after a bit she couldn't take the killings.'

Coffin found he believed her.

'She was still frightened, but she knew I'd do my best for her.'

He nodded at Phoebe as they turned towards her car. Then he said to Inspector Ardet. 'As you have done, Winnie. I reckon you've been a good friend.'

'What do you make of that?' he asked Phoebe as they drove off. 'Did Owner hear what she claims?'

'I think so. Not what I'd call an inventive woman.'

'No. But a frightened one.' He watched as Phoebe swung the car into the busy traffic. 'Wonder what's she frightened of?'

'Well, she said: the serial killer.'

'Is that enough?'

'It might be,' said Phoebe who thought it very well would be for her if she was in Mrs Owner's (what a name!) position. Of course, as a serving police officer she was often in a worse position but backed up and supported by her mates. That did help.

Layers here, Coffin thought, complicated layers, it was often the way with a murder case. Sometimes you could never see straight through to the bottom. It was hard to live with that, but you had to learn how.

'What she seemed to hear, or perhaps I should say what she seemed to make of the dying woman's words, was that she was a stand in or substitute.'

'Theatrical,' said Coffin shortly. 'The understudy.'

So who was the star?

'I know you think this connects with Miss Pinero somehow.'

'Not just think,' said Coffin fiercely. 'I *know*.'

Phoebe drove on in silence. Some very strange thoughts were milling around in her head. How could Stella be part of this? And yet Stella already was. She had been attacked, kidnapped, and only escaped by a kind of miracle. Phoebe hardly knew what to say. 'Straight home, sir,' was all she managed. 'Or back to HQ?'

'I'll go to the theatre and see Stella.'

'Right, sir, right.'

'But take me to the Tower first, I must look in on the cat again. He doesn't like being left. Not for too long.'

He stepped out of the car quickly. 'Thanks, Phoebe. You get back to work.'

'Yes, sir. Anything specially you'd like me to do?' She didn't expect much of an answer, but she didn't want to leave him with that look on his face.

'Only catch the bugger, Phoebe.'

'Do my best, sir.'

She drove off, in her own car. There seemed a lot of activity round one side of the theatre... some trouble with the foundation of the new building she supposed, but she didn't pay much attention, there was too much else to think about.

Coffin let himself in, his home was quiet, even the cat was asleep, although a flick of the animal's tail hinted that he might be willing to wake up.

He sank into a chair to think things over. In a little while he would go over to the theatre to find Stella.

'Have a drink,' he told himself, but he did not move. Alcohol would not solve his worries. 'I'm not pushing the teams as I should. Maybe I should call in the Met.'

He stood up and started to walk round the room. 'God, I'd hate to do that...I know who will come in with all his cohorts: Archy Bledlow. Archy bloody Bledlow. Archie with his Bond Street hair cut and his forensic scientist that he always seems to have in his pocket.'

The thought of how much he would hate it stiffened him. 'Straighten yourself, Coffin. You can do it.'

Now *was* the moment for a drink, so he went in search of a bottle that suited his mood. The ginger cat just opened an eye but did not move, waiting to see what would happen, having unconsciously adopted the safe way of life; letting someone else (preferably the dog) take the first step, fall for whatever trouble there was, and wait to see what good for a cat would come of it all.

Coffin poured himself a drink. Red wine, had to be red wine, he felt his blood needed warming. Or thinning.

He needed some strength behind. There was Paul Masters, the supreme administrator, no one better at a filing system, but a well-ordered filing cabinet was not always the answer to everything. There was Phoebe Astley, he could rely on Phoebe. Not too strong on imagination, but that could be a virtue.

Then there was Les Henderson. He liked the lad, a lot of potential there. He meant to bring him on, and this case might offer the opportunity. Might be a good idea to find out a bit more about Henderson. The official record he knew, of course: started with the uniformed branch, did his stint plodding the beat, transferred to the detection arm, rapid promotion at the same time as taking a degree in the Open University (got a good second class), a good Catholic, unmarried, popular with his colleagues.

Must have some faults, Coffin thought. Knowledge of which would certainly come Coffin's way sooner or later. No doubt Phoebe knew and would tell if asked. 'Doesn't fancy me,' she might say, which would certainly rate as a real sin in Phoebe's eyes, although no doubt not in that of the young detective's father confessor. He'd have enjoyed a son like Henderson although he doubted if the lad would have wanted a father like him. His own itinerant mother and absent father had hardly been a good training in parenting.

Coffin went to get another drink, but decided to ring the Incident Room first. It was more than one room, in fact, as was necessary with an investigation of this size. A well-oiled machine, which sometimes in a case he ignored, but which now he felt the need of for the support it offered.

Inspector Peter Beatty who was in charge (in as much as anyone was since officers were moving in and out on their own ploys all the time, sometime speaking, sometimes not), put down his mug of coffee to answer the Chief Commander. Instinct had told him it was the boss figure otherwise he might have let it ring longer whilst he finished the notes he was looking at.

'No sir, no special developments.'

Across his desk, his second phone was ringing. No news there either, he decided sadly.

Wrongly, as it happened.

Coffin accepted what he said, with a sigh, then went to get his drink. The cat's ears went up.

'Hello, you. Woke you up, did I?'

The cat sat up, listening.

Then Coffin too heard something.

A moment later Stella came running up the winding staircase and burst into the room. She flung herself towards her husband. 'Oh my darling... I'm so glad you are here. Something terrible!'

Chapter 11

Stella threw her arms around her husband.

'Bless you. What a convenient person you are.'

'Am I?' Coffin was surprised, he hoped it was a compliment.

'Oh yes, always there when you are wanted.'

I suppose that's a good thing to be, thought Coffin, but he enjoyed the feeling of Stella in his arms and he hugged her.

'I mean you don't go pissing around,' she murmured into his shoulder,' you're there, when wanted.'

'So come on, love. Tell me what is this new horror. Not another murdered woman?'

'No... well, I don't know. Dead, but who did what I don't know... there are three of them, you see. At the theatre.'

Coffin dropped his arms and drew away from her. 'I'd better come to see for myself.'

'I haven't explained very well.'

'No.' He voice was still tender, but stern at the same time: this was work.

Stella knew this side of him of old and respected it without enjoying it.

'I'm going across to see what is happening. You can come with me and tell me what you know. As we walk. Also,' he added thoughtfully, 'how you got dragged into it.'

'It *is* my theatre,' said Stella, as she followed him down the stairs. After them came Gus, determined to be part of the team, watched from the top of the staircase by the cat. 'But it was Robbie Lightsett really...'

Robbie Lightsett (he hated his name but he had never seen any way round it) knew that getting this construction job of the new theatre had been a great triumph. Added to which he was a fan of Stella Pinero. 'Not so much she's lovely to look at, but she's a marvellous actress and such charm,' he said to his wife, who thankfully was not a jealous woman. 'Actresses know how to make up,' observed his wife, who although not jealous was sharp eyed.

Robbie and his team of workers were clearing the ground for the foundations of the building. It meant digging up some ancient gardens which had once run up to the edge of St Luke's when it had been just a church - now it was a scrubby area used as an extra car park. 'Waste ground,' Stella had pronounced it as she showed round the banker who was going to lend her the money to build. Banking was only one of his professions but owning millions deserved a good name. He also loved the theatre and was not, so he said, going to be greedy about interest on the loan. This would be the fourth theatre on the site, possibly dedicated to TV drama; tiny, but very fashionable and popular: as benefactor, he hoped to get a knighthood out of it. Maybe even a peerage?

Robbie had four men working for him clearing the ground and digging, all four were good and trusted workers so he himself did not stay around all day as he had another job on the go in Spinnergate.

It was quite by chance that he walked on to the site when they found the first body.

Then the second, and finally the third.

He was glad he was there, it was his job to be there, but he could not pretend it had been a good moment.

Startling and alarming, yes.

He knew the minute he saw Alfie Goode's face that something really bad had happened.

'What's up, Alfie?' he shouted as he moved forward rapidly. Alfie was the one who could put problems into words, make coherent sentences of them, even write a report if he had to which was why he was foreman, although tiny little Mark was the better craftsman. Mark was standing behind Alfie, while behind Mark was Minnie, his wife and fellow worker who could shift a spade-full with anyone. Probably carry Mark off over her shoulder, which rumour had it she had indeed done. On their wedding day too. She spoke rarely when at work, but had a good vocabulary when she did.

'Sir, sir!' Alfie was saying, his face a picture of horror. Since he was not a man who showed emotion much, Robbie called out not to worry, he was coming. 'Could hardly believe it, sir... we were clearing the ground for the men to come in and set the foundations...' Robby employed subcontractors for certain operations '...and the architect was going to come. She's there now.'

'Yes, I can see her,' said Robbie. Stella felt strongly about the position of professional women so she always employed a woman if she could. Robbie, who felt at heart that women were best in the kitchen and in the bed, had eventually come to accept it. Any man employed by Stella Pinero was bound to come to that conclusion in the end.

Robbie had got to the diggings so that he could stare down into the pit.

Grave was more the word to call it.

'They've been buried here,' he said incredulously.

'They sure as hell didn't crawl into the hole and draw the earth in after them,' said Alfie. Behind him his silent supporters lined up, staring into the grave.

Robbie got down on his knees for a closer look. There were three figures. Some quality of the earth had mummified the bodies without entirely reducing them to skeletons. Some remnants of clothing clung to each body.

The evidence suggested that here they had a man, a woman, and a child.

'We'll have to call the police,' said Alfie.

'We can leave that to Miss Pinero, I reckon. We can trust to that with her connections.'

The architect, D.H. Armour, (she always used only her initials, neutral) came over to where they were. D.H. Armour was a tall, beautifully dressed woman, carrying her trademark briefcase.

'My God, what have you turned up?'

No one answered since all was to be seen at a glance.

'They look very young,' she said, her voice suddenly tender.

'How can you tell?' asked Robbie.

'By the clothes, what's left of them, they're kids clothes.'

It was at this moment that Stella Pinero arrived. She came over to see what they were all staring at, then drew in her breath sharply.

'We thought you might tell your husband,' said Robbie.

Coffin and Stella arrived together, he had his arm round Stella who looked composed. What a handy, calming thing is a husband, Stella was thinking, John really helps me through a crisis. I must do the same for him.

Accordingly, she brushed her cheek against her husband and said: 'Love you, darling.'

He grinned back. 'Actress.'

Oh good, she thought, I got it right. Aloud, she said: 'Actor, dear, we're all actors these days.'

Thus fortified, they went to look at the dead ones.

Coffin drew in his breath.

'It certainly looks like murder, anyway, it's got to be cleared up,' he said in a sombre voice. 'I'll have to summon up a complete investigating team.' His mind was running over pathologists and forensic scientists.

'Who will you put in charge?'

'I'll have to leave that to the CID outfit. They're pretty stretched at the moment.' Chief Superintendent Bart Brewer was in charge there, a man promoted beyond his powers and already showing signs of strain. Not that Coffin could blame him, he was feeling the strain himself. How he wished he still had Archie Young at his side. But his well deserved promotion had taken Archie away then his beloved son who had been working in the Second City Force had been killed.

What misery and anxieties I might have could not compare with yours, Archie, I respect that.

'These deaths... they can't have any connections with the serial murders that are happening now, can they?' asked Stella.

Robbie listened intently, as did Alfie and his acolytes.

'No,' said Coffin thoughtfully. 'I don't think so.'

Stella was silent for a bit, listening while Coffin spoke on his mobile phone. She heard the directions he was giving: Press and TV to be kept out.

'I suppose it won't be necessary to cancel the evening performance?'

Although her voice was diffident and gentle, Coffin knew it would be a strong anxiety. That was the theatre, he thought: the show must go on.

'I must leave that decision to the officer in charge, but I think that if the area is roped off and a guard set up, you can go ahead.'

He knew very well that it was his decision that would count and that he would do his best for Stella. She knew it too. He could see it in her eyes. They allowed themselves a faint, very faint smile.

'Thanks,' she breathed. 'Financially, we're a bit on a knife edge at the moment.'

They always were, of course, but they always carried on one way or another and Stella would see they did now.

'Won't do anything you don't approve,' she said.

'Of course you won't.'

He took another look at the trio of the dead, neatly arranged according to size.

Someone must have known who they were. So they must have been reported missing.

And if not, why not.

Was that a question, he asked himself, or a statement?

'Who did you call? Or shouldn't I ask?'

'I asked for Phoebe Astley to speak to me. As to whether

she handles it or not, we'll have to see. Bart Brewer may have other ideas...'

But he intended Phoebe should. These deaths meant digging into the past and Phoebe was good at that.

D.H. Armour said: 'I suppose I might as well get off, Miss Pinero? I guess the building won't make much progress for a while.'

Robbie and Co. were already packing up while waiting for their dismissal.

'I'm afraid so,' Stella said to the architect. 'I am sorry if your time has been wasted.'

'Not exactly wasted. It's not been without interest. They were only kids, you know, and the little one...' She shook her head. 'A baby. Killed, poor little soul, just as an extra.'

'Is that how you see it?' Stella asked.

D.H. Armour shrugged. She was trying to listen to what Coffin, on his mobile again, was saying. But she couldn't catch anything. Well, perhaps a word or two.

She thought she caught the word Phoebe, she had met DCI Astley once and though in general a supporter of ambitious professional woman, she had not taken to Phoebe Astley. Jealousy, she told herself honestly, at heart I am a bloody dinosaur.

'Phoebe, I want you to have this one... I'll fix it with Bart.' Coffin had summoned Phoebe to his office and now was meeting her there, with Paul Masters hovering in the background. He had taken in lately that Phoebe Astley was going up in the guvnor's estimation and was not sure if he liked it. He liked Phoebe herself though, and knew she was clever. Jealousy, he was also admitting to himself, not knowing D.H. Armour had been thinking herself guilty of the same. With a suddenness that was almost pain, he realised that he liked Phoebe a good deal more than he had realised and the feeling was getting stronger. Phoebe, he thought, you and I have a way to go together if you agree.

Phoebe started to say something. She could tell from Coffin's voice, always under control but whose tones she had learnt to read, that he was anxious. He always was where Stella was concerned and certainly she was a lady who attracted trouble. Perhaps actresses were all like that.

'You've only got the mannequin, haven't you? I mean with all that goes with it. How are you getting on with that? Any progress?' The mannequin had been the beginning. Or one of the beginnings, he thought savagely.

'I'm handling the murders as well and Mercy's gone sick,' said Phoebe in a level voice.

Coffin nodded. 'So I was told.' Their eyes met, but nothing was said.

'We could do with Joe back. I'd like to know what he'd make of it all.'

'So?' queried Coffin. 'What do *you* make of it? The whole set of events? You don't want to say, do you? Not even about the mannequin?'

'It's all a bit intangible,' she admitted. In fact, the source of the mannequin had not yet been traced. Originally it came from a theatrical supplier in Windsor who manufactured them but they were still tracking where this particular one may have been bought from.

'I think this case might be described as intangible too,' said Coffin grimly.

'I'd like to report more progress, sir. With all this other business going on, the series of killings, it doesn't seem so important, maybe. It's only that the dummy seemed to touch Miss Pinero.'

'This case might too.'

'That's a bit tortuous, sir.' Phoebe was always very careful to call Coffin sir when she was disagreeing with him.

But was she disagreeing with him? The truth was that she had not as yet even visited the scene of the three bodies just uncovered. A vivid description by Coffin was not enough, she thought, until she had had a chance to see them. It is not the sort of murder that I am good at solving, she told herself savagely. What I should like is a straightforward, open-and-shut case where a chap is killed with a hammer to the head by his next door neighbour and you know it's because he is having an affair with the neighbour's wife. That's my sort of murder, you know where you are with one like that. I'm a plain detective, not a fancy one. His lordship there is the fancy one.

The "fancy one" was still talking at her. About Stella, of course.

'Well, sir...' she began.

'It's her theatre. Or will be. The ground's hers. Or the lease is.'

'What are you saying, sir?'

'It seems to touch my wife again,' he said with a groan. 'I don't like it. '

'I don't see it, sir.' But Phoebe said it reluctantly, she knew her boss well enough to trust his intuitions.

Coffin ignored this comment and went on:

'When the scientific boys work out how long the bodies have been there, let me know.' More and more they were relying on the scientists. Even crime was getting technical.

'It's important to find out how long these bodies have been there, and who they are.'

'I agree.'

'Anything new on the serial killer?'

She shook her head. 'No.'

'The press will be howling like hyenas... I don't know why they haven't been already.'

'I know,' ventured Phoebe. 'It's the royal divorce. They want all the news space they can get.'

'I didn't know there was one.'

'Oh, there will be. Bound to be.'

If she hoped for a laugh she didn't get one. Coffin went on:

'And when you've finished work today, you might pop in and see Mercy.'

Phoebe nodded. 'Will do.'

'I think she might be worried about Joe. I am too. I had a word with his doctor but he didn't say much.'

Phoebe didn't go straight away at the end of the day. First, she wanted to talk to the rest of her colleagues handling the serial killings.

Before that she had spoken on the phone to the forensic and pathologists involved.

She got on to the forensic experts first to prod them on.

Phoebe knew that it was hopeless to ask for quick answers from the two scientists in charge, because, as they had told her often in the past, their work by its very nature was slow and methodical.

But she could try.

'Well, Dickie' she said to the forensic expert, 'Get a move on, please.'

'We're in the same fight here, you know. And it's Dickon, not Dickie,'

'Sounds Anglo-Saxon... Chaucer? Or Shakespeare?'

'It's a family name, and both Chaucer and Shakespeare were English but not Anglo- Saxon.' He knew she was baiting him but could not help rising to it. The trouble with forensic medicine was that it was a humourless business. Pathology, might just be one degree worse, she judged.

Dr Death, Phoebe called the pathologist Hugh Meldrum, but she had to admit that Dr Meldrum, young and a new recruit to the Second City Police as very junior pathologist, was easier to talk to than Dickon. He would produce a bit of information, because he always did. He handed over these snippets of information like polished pearls, then sat back to wait for her response.

'So what have you got for me?'

'It's very early, too soon to speak with authority.' Nevertheless, he would do so. He always did. 'So handle with care. ' He added his usual rider.

'Well, come on, please. Let me have your first thoughts.' She tried not to sound hurried since this irritated Meldrum who did not like his pearls spat upon.

'There are three bodies.' He paused: a pearl was coming.

'Right.' This was to hurry him up.

'A young male, fully extended, on his left side a female, likewise at full stretch, she is also young, and on her left, an infant. You understand this is just from my first superficial inspection?'

'Of course.' She could tell that a real, natural pearl was about to appear, nothing cultured.

'The girl was strangled, the baby was smothered and as far as I can tell before a post mortem, the lad was poisoned.' He became portentous. 'And before you ask, I cannot as yet say what the poison was. Or how it was administered.' He added 'But it *may* have been self-administered. His body bears no signs of violence...'

'Are you suggesting that he killed his companions, then committed suicide?' said Phoebe.

'And then lay down and drew the earth over the three of them? That *would* be an interesting case.' Meldrum remarked drily.

'It's that already,' said Phoebe, with feeling.

She frowned as she settled at her desk and considered the situation. She never knew if he was laughing at her or not.

Phoebe picked up the telephone, but no one she wanted to speak to seemed to be at their desk.

Her next port of call was a corner of the canteen where she had pleaded with all those officers dealing with the serial murders to come to an impromptu meeting. If they could manage it.

She had chosen this spot rather than the small briefing room where they could have met as being more informal.

They could manage it.

Coffin's name, which she had used, was powerful.

From the door she totted up who she had got. Les

Henderson, next to him Inspector Winnie Ardet, and even Superintendent Miller. Not a bad tally, she'd got the most important.

'All present and correct,' she said lightly. Then, sensing that this did not go down well, 'thanks for coming.'

'Think we'd dare not?' This was Winnie.

Sometimes, oh sometimes, said Phoebe to herself, I sense not everyone likes me very much.

'We've all got plenty on our plate with the serial killer on our patch.'

'If it *is* just the one killer,' said Winnie.

'If it is, but I think its probable.' Phoebe smiled at Winnie. To her relief, Winnie smiled back.

'No real evidence, he's a clever bugger. You'd think he was the invisible man, the way he manages to leave no forensic traces. None,' she said with real feeling.

'So what do you want from us?' asked Sergeant Henderson. 'What can we do for you? I know you won't think me cynical if I believe you aren't planning to do anything for us? No sudden revelations or confessions that we ought to hear?' as Phoebe shook her head. 'No, I thought not, love, so out with it.'

Phoebe stood up. 'Let's have a drink while we talk. I'm sure you all want one. No, I'll do it, I called this meeting.' She knew her colleagues well enough to know what they wanted to drink. Les would want beer, Winnie a dry white wine, and Miller would have coffee with her.

She looked at Les and he rose politely to help her carry the drinks.

'So what are we playing at?' he asked.

'No game Les.'

When they got back to the table she ran quickly through what had happened from the beginning: the messages, the strange figure of the mannequin woman, the attack on Stella. Parallel with all this in time were the serial murders. And little Charlie Fisher, the killing that she could make no sense of.

Her audience listened without comment.

Glad I provided the drinks, she thought, or they wouldn't know what to do.

'The Chief Commander thinks it is all, somehow, aimed at Stella.'

She got no applause but a moment of silence. Then Winnie said: 'She's certainly a lady that knows how to get into trouble, we've seen it in the past, but I don't think even she would arrange all this just for publicity.'

Phoebe ignored this. 'And now three bodies have been discovered on the site of the new theatre.'

Into the silence, Les muttered: 'Had heard a little something. Better go and take a look.'

'May not be easy, there should be a tent over it by now and the whole area fenced off, I ordered it. Oh, and Les, if you go inside, but I'd prefer you didn't, protective clothing, boots and gloves, please.'

'I know the rules.'

'Just reminding you.'

'Were they killed on the spot?'

'No.' Phoebe felt sure of herself here.

'Then that's not how our serial killer works: he kills and walks away. And three bodies, did you say? He's never done three at one go.'

'Who's your SOCO?' asked Superintendent Miller, always the professional.

'We soon won't have enough officers left free to have a Scene of the Crime Officer for every murder,' grumbled Les.

'We all know that you will have done everything the right way,' said Winnie. 'God you knows you've had enough practice, we all have. '

'Thanks, Winnie.'

'But I think we are all beginning to feel a bit sick.'

'All I am asking, and it's what the Chief Commander wants, is to find out where Stella comes in. Well, that's it, friends, thank you for coming.'

'It's back to work,' said Les, leading the exit. 'I don't know if what you and the Chief Commander have brewed up helps or not.'

Phoebe thought she did not know either.

As she walked across the canteen and then out into the corridor which led to the car park, she saw Coffin. She held back as he went to his car.

He was walking in that head down, purposeful way that usually meant a problem elsewhere.

Well, he had plenty of those, but where was he going now?

Phoebe knew him well enough to feel a sense of disquiet.

But she also knew where she had to go and that was to see Mercy Adams. She knew where Mercy lived - at least she knew the address although she had never been there. After Mercy's second husband died, she went back to live in the family home with her children. A flat was carved out for her on the top two floors of the largish old house where she had grown up. She felt happy there, she had told Phoebe, and having her own establishment had kept family relationships peaceful.

She walked up to the door, pressed the bell which said Adams, then waited.

No one came. So she pressed it again. This time, she heard footsteps coming towards the door, so she got her face ready to smile at Mercy with gentle sympathy and not too much enquiry.

But it was Mercy's mother who opened the door.

'Can I speak to Mercy? I'm Phoebe Astley, we work together.'

'Oh yes, I know you dear.' She held the door open more widely so that Phoebe stepped into the hall which smelt of furniture polish and lavender. 'I don't want to disturb her, dear, she's had a terrible migraine and I think she's just dropped off. Some other time?'

'Yes, of course. Will you tell her I called and give her my

sympathy... I know how painful migraine can be. I've had it myself sometimes.'

'It's tension, I think, don't you?'

'Her doctor could help, I expect. There are some drugs that work for migraine for most people.'

'Oh yes, I'll see she goes once she's safe to walk around. You look after yourself too, dear.'

'Oh I do, I do,' Phoebe assured her, thinking that Mercy's mother was a candidate for a soothing potion herself.

As she got into her car to drive off, she turned her head to see if all was clear behind before moving out. Just coming into view at top of the road, was a figure she could swear was Mercy's.

As she sat there, debating whether to get out and run to greet Mercy, she saw the figure turn round and disappear round the corner.

Recognised the car? What about that rumour that she had had an abortion and doesn't want to talk about it? With someone like Mercy you could never tell. Perhaps it had more to do with that young doctor of hers?

She drove off slowly. What the hell was happening?

Chapter 12

When you are a man with a taste for killing then murder is the ultimate refreshment.

It should not be so, the murderer, in his way a highly moral man, knew this but had to admit the pleasure.

He had, as all good performers must have, a props room where he kept all that was needed for his performances. It was in an old garage not so far away from Mimsie Marker's stall and next door to the Catholic Church. He often had a conversation with Father McPartlin. He enjoyed meeting him although he had to be very careful what he said and what face he turned towards him.

A sharp observer, Father McPartlin. Well, it stood to reason, you could not survive as a parson in the Second City without a strong heart and stronger reason, so Father McPartlin had certainly observed that he wore a wig and that his head underneath it was as shiny bald as an egg. Too kindly and polite to mention anything. You could get good wigs that, apparently, could not be told from real but they were very expensive, and why waste money? Personally he thought this one suited him, made him feel quite boyish. But the curls tickled.

He took his wig off, with the Father watching, and shook his head. 'Bit warm today.'

'It is, it is... Do you know, I think your hair is growing back.'

'Is it? The doctors said it might.' He was indifferent.

'Which hospital do you attend?'

Lovely prissy way of talking, the father had.

'The University Hospital.'

'You don't mind me asking? My intention is kindly.'

Of course, it is, loving kindness is your business. Mine is hate.

'Not at all, Father.' Besides, I don't have to tell the truth. Nor do I. He could feel a comfortable, warm bubble of hate springing up inside him. He had no use for it at the moment but it was good to feel it was there if he needed it.

He went back inside, making things tidy. He hung up several garments, then he inspected two pairs of shoes. They must be polished. No stains anywhere, though. Remarkable that, but of course, he knew what to do.

Presently, his attention was claimed by voices from outside on the steps to the church He put his ear to the wall to listen.

Mimsie Marker's strong tones penetrated where he was standing, thinking about life. And death.

'Here are your sandwiches, Father. Made them myself, they are good but you ought to eat properly, Father.'

'Your sandwiches are very nourishing, Mimsie.'

'Not like good hot roast beef, Father, or a lamb chop or two... or fish on the right day. It's not one of those starvation days today, is it?'

'No, not today, Mimsie.'

'Good, because you've got grilled bacon in those sandwiches.'

The voices fell away at that point so he could hear no more. Then by careful attention he could hear them again. Discussing his favourite subject.

The killings.

'I hope you are taking care, Mimsie, when you go around... these murders...'

'Don't worry about me, Father. I can look after myself. I always have a heavy walking stick in my hand and a knife in my pocket... I know how to use it, too.'

'So does the murderer, Mimsie.' He added, 'Of course, you can always go home in your Rolls.'

'I do *not* have a Rolls, Father,' said Mimsie severely, ' that is a total fabrication.'

The killer murmured to himself that Mimsie was safe, she was not in his killing market. 'Of course, if you are keen, then I will try to fit you on to the list.'

But no, there was no response from the little bubble of anger and hate inside him, so Mimsie was certainly safe.

He went back to tidying up the garments, all of which he would take home to wash. It was true, as he knew, that forensic scientists could pick up traces of blood and other matters on an article of clothing that had been washed, but he also knew that modern detergents and bleaches could seriously decompose such traces.

Mimsie Marker (who in his opinion ought to be getting back to her stall) and the Father were still talking .'No, there is no description of the killer that I've heard,' she was saying.

No, of course, you wouldn't have heard. Who do you think you are? thought the killer.

'And if there had been one, then you can bet that one of my customers would have passed it on to me. I get a lot of important police officers coming along for a paper and perhaps a drink before they catch a train across the river.'

The killer ground his teeth in anger. She might be correct, some officers knew how to talk, all right, and over a hot coffee and a sandwich might well do so.

He got on with his work, his mood still sour. Mimsie must have gone and the Father be off eating his bacon sandwiches because all was quiet.

Then once more he could hear a conversation floating in from the street. Two women this time.

'Oh she's so lovely.'

Not a voice he recognised.

'I go see almost every play she's in. Not the very highbrow or tragic ones. She's always good, our dear Stella Pinero but to my mind she's at her best in comedy.'

'I agree. But I do like her in Shakespeare. But you can't call Shakespeare highbrow, can you?'

No, you can't, you cow, he thought, putting his eye to a crack in the door. No one he knew. Middle-aged, both of them. Well dressed, one in a red suit, the other in black, wearing a bit of jewellery, hair seen to by a good hairdresser. Not on the game. But he had known that from the snatch of conversation. There might be a few toms who appreciated the acting of Stella Pinero but in his experience nary a one that liked Shakespeare. Funny that, because they must have done once when the first Globe theatre was building. One of the best places in Tudor London to tout for custom, he wouldn't mind betting.

Wasn't that how Nell Gwynne started out?

He heard the name Stella again, and the bubble of anger inside him grew into a great balloon. One that swelled and pulsated.

It had Stella Pinero's face on it.

There was a red balloon hanging from a string on a hook on the wall on which some unskilled hand had drawn eyes, a nose, and mouth.

He drew his hand up and down the pretend head. 'Oh Stella, you little know.' He stood looking at the plastic face. 'You think you've been through it and escaped. That is so, isn't it?' He took a deep breath. 'That was only a rehearsal, Miss Pinero. You know what a rehearsal is, don't you? A forerunner to the *real* performance.'

Father McPartlin was quiet, and the street outside was empty.

He stroked the plastic face again, almost with affection. ' I wish I could trust you to react with fear the way you should, but you are one tough lady.' He pushed the face away, so that it swung on its cord. 'I shall have to work on that.' He gave the face a hard slap, then walked away.

He had left his mobile phone on the table in the middle of the room. On this table he piled things that did not matter like old newspapers and empty plastic bags from big stores, all anonymous stuff, so that if anyone discovered his secret hidey-hole they would not get much profit from what lay around. It would be discovered in the end. Nothing was a secret for ever in his experience but he planned not to be there then. Move on, and out, that was his plan. Yes, they would pick up a few fingerprints from the plastic bags and even the table itself, but so what? He did not care.

He knew he would be found out as the killer, sooner or later. He wanted to be.

At the end, he wanted Stella Pinero to know all.

He tapped out a number on the mobile and waited for an answer. One came eventually but he knew to wait.

'Hello. I was busy.'

'Of course. Well, there you are.'

Conversation between the two was never easy. It was hard to know why since on many issues their views were the same. Just bad communicators, he supposed. Yet in his profession, such as it was, he should be a good one.

'I wanted to let you know that you had a call from that young woman who is keen on you.'

'A call in person? Or the phone?'

'Telephone. I told her you would get in touch.'

'I suppose I had better.'

'I think so, she sounded distressed.'

'She's got worries, poor woman.'

'Haven't we all?'

There was so much truth in this that a silence fell. Then he muttered something about the hospital.

'Oh yes, the bloody hospital,' came the even lower mutter in reply.

Chapter 13

Phoebe, knowing the duties of her job, made a report of all she had done to the Chief Commander. As she typed it out she wished she had a lover, a man to pour it all out to in bed, but there was no one around at the moment. Her own fault, no doubt. Anyway, it would have to be another officer of high rank to pass on such information or the Chief Commander would go ballistic.

Might do so anyway since anything connected with Stella made him anxious. Quite right too, Stella was exciting, a compelling actress, but... and there was a but, she could be a flaming nuisance.

But it was not primarily Stella about whom Phoebe thought she must consult the Chief Commander, although naturally she came into it (whenever was Stella out of anything?). Phoebe allowed herself this touch of asperity which she recognised was just jealousy. (Jealous of Stella? she asked herself severely, goodness knows. Well, envious maybe.) There were other things on Phoebe's mind.

She sat looking at what she had typed, then walked away from it. Perhaps she should not deliver it just yet.

Looked at coldly, it was just full of vague disquiet. All of which she certainly felt, as, she was coming to believe, did the Chief Commander. The trouble was that she had known him a long while, even before she came to the Second City, and their minds seemed to work in the same way. They were often right together but they could also be wrong together.

It might be more sensible to talk to Mercy first, find out why she had sloped off. A firm hand is all that is needed. Mercy, I'll say, what the hell were you doing out walking when you were said to be prostrate with migraine. This case needs you.

'Come on, Mercy,' she muttered as the phone rang. No

answer. Either not there or not answering. The answerphone voice muttered something which Phoebe ignored.

She then tried the downstairs apartment of her house hoping to get Mercy's mother. She answered at once, as if she was waiting for a call. Still, she might have been that sort of woman. I'm often eager myself, Phoebe thought. Usually a work reason these days, lovers being short on the ground.

'This is Phoebe Astley. Mercy's not answering. Is she there?'

There was a pause.

'Well, she should be,' said her mother at length.

'That's what I thought.'

'She may be still asleep... she sleeps late these days. And it is early.'

' I would like to talk to her. Could you see?'

'She may have gone out, we don't watch each other... Do forgive me, someone at my door.'

Mercy's not there and Mum knows it and won't say. Whatever was up, Phoebe was irritated.

More. 'I'm worried,' she said aloud. 'If Mercy knows something about this terrible series of events that I don't know, and the rest of the team don't know, not to mention Coffin, then she ought to tell us.'

Although Phoebe knew John Coffin as a friend she knew protocol: you approached Sir John through Paul Masters. The Chief Commander certainly had secretaries, two or three at a time with carefully distributed duties but even in John Coffin's stable life secretaries came and went: got married, had babies (not necessarily in that order), moved to Australia - one had even won a large sum on the Lottery - but Paul Masters seemed unlikely to do any of these things.

Phoebe did not mind telephoning Paul although she had had a run-in or two with him herself in the past, but in the end it seemed best to go to see him.

'I'd really like you to have a talk with him. He was trying himself to get into touch with one of the officers working on these serial killings... Sergeant Adams, I think.'

'I wonder why he wanted to talk to her?' As Phoebe did herself.

'Because she seemed to be out of touch,' said Paul tersely. 'Sir doesn't care for that. Not with a serial killer on the loose. I don't suppose he thinks she'll solve it but he wants everyone on parade. ' To friends and equals he allowed himself to show a flash of sharpness even about John Coffin whom he much admired. But it always came with a smile. As now.

At this moment Coffin himself strode into the office. He seemed pleased to see Phoebe Astley.

'Any progress on the three bodies?'

'At the moment it looks as though the young man killed the girl and the baby and then took poison.'

'He didn't bury himself, though,'

'No. Someone else did that for him.'

'Or that someone killed all three then buried them. Seems more likely to me. You don't go round burying bodies as you find them.'

'I don't know,' said Phoebe. 'A funny business altogether, except I'm not laughing.'

'We're going to suffer a Public Enquiry into why we haven't cleared these cases.' Coffin shook his head. 'I can feel it in the air. And after that will come the execution.'

He pulled a long face, and then gave a grin as he walked on and out through the door which led to his private sanctum. You had to be invited into there. Usually a dog in there and on occasion a cat as well.

'You can't get him down,' said Paul Masters with admiration. Phoebe looked thoughtful. 'I reckon he knows something we don't', she said quietly.

Paul Masters questioned: 'Do you know anything or are you just guessing?'

'Just guessing,' said Phoebe sadly.

At the door, Coffin paused and turned his head. ' I am out to see my wife: she says she thinks she recognises the dead young man found with the three bodies. He was a would-be actor who did not get a place in the training scheme for the theatre.' He added. 'Stella's good on faces, in her position she has to be.'

'Can I interview Lady Coffin, sir?' asked Phoebe quickly.

'If she says yes, then you certainly can and must interview her, but let me go first, and a word in your ear: she prefers Pinero to Coffin... well, who wouldn't?'

'Thank you, sir,' said Phoebe ironically as he disappeared.

'He's right,' Paul Masters spoke up in support of his boss. 'If he thinks there's something in it, then you'll get first dip.'

'I wonder why she didn't say something before?' queried Phoebe.

'Why didn't you tell me this before?' Coffin asked his wife.

'Because I had to clear my own mind, make certain I did recognise him.'

'And you are sure?'

Stella nodded. She had asked Coffin to come to her office in the theatre where Gus sat on her feet, looking up at Coffin. You felt he could never decide which of the two he loved most.

Stella was drinking coffee, hot and fragrant as it would have to be to meet her high standards. In her youth she had drunk too much of what she called "backstage" coffee, weak and cool, to accept anything but the best now. 'Want a cup?'

She would want something stronger than coffee after a good look at the body now stretched out in a cold drawer in the morgue.

'No, drink it up and let's get you down to see if you can identify the body.'

'I did have a quick look when he was found. That's when I thought I knew him, poor boy'

'Now you can have a longer look.'

Stella was silent as Coffin drove her to the police morgue, silent as the drawer was dragged out so that she could look.

She stared for a moment in silence. Even with the contractions and stains of death on the features, she knew him.

She nodded silently to Coffin, then stepped back. He took her arm. What had happened was getting to her.

'Let's go and have a drink and talk. Your coffee is marvellous but I fancy a change of scene.'

Without consulting Stella, he drove her to Cafe Blanc, in a side road not far from Mimsie Marker's stall. He strongly suspected that the establishment was a part of Mimsie's empire. There was something in the style of food and the presentation of it, and the smiling confidence with which she recommended it.

He found a table for two by the window, sat Stella down at it, and ordered a bottle of wine.

'Drink up. You need it.' He poured. 'Red wine. You're pale, it'll do you good.'

Stella picked up the glass. 'How pale do I have to be to get champagne?'

Coffin laughed. 'Worse than you are now. Come on, drink up, my love.'

Stella drank some wine, and the colour began to come back into her cheeks. Then she began to talk.

'He was one of the boys in the competition for a prize and a place in the company: as I remember he was called Robert something - I can look it up. Eglin, I think it was. He was very, very keen, he got through several rounds in which people were eliminated. But he was up against very stiff competition and the final winner was a lad, Andrew Eliot... extremely good, unusual style too.'

'I think I've seen him,' said Coffin.

'You might well have seen him around... red hair and a pale face, but hasn't performed in public yet. Nor will he for some time... I am taking some of the classes myself, but the donation we were given has allowed me to hire a teacher from RADA. He was glad to come too, bit of extra experience.'

Stella was talking too much and she knew it.

'And Robert?' Coffin reminded her.

'I don't know... never saw him again, until... It's a harsh profession, the stage.'

Into the pause, Coffin said: 'He may have killed himself, he may have killed the girl and child, but he did not bury all of them... So that means at least one other person knows about his death.'

Stella said: 'My office may still have his address... last address that is, and a few personal details... I think he hung around a bit afterwards. And the boy who won may know more... the young and hopeful do tend to chum up a bit.'

'I'll talk to him. Or may be Phoebe could.'

'She can be a bit alarming... Mercy might be better.'

'I want to talk to Mercy myself,' said Coffin grimly. The difficulty of making contact with Mercy, one of the team he had set up to deal with the serial killer, had been irritating him. Unwell she might be, absent was not allowed.

He made a decision. 'I'll talk to the lad myself... with your help, Stella.'

'Andy Eliot?' said Stella. 'He's around. I saw him flitting about in the distance this morning.' She added, thoughtfully: 'He's a lovely boy, a lot of potential. I hope we can help bring all that talent into play.'

If Coffin caught the hesitation in her tone he did not show it.

Andrew Eliot was not a conventionally handsome boy, but his face was interesting and alert. Coffin knew enough about the stage by now to know that this was an actor's face, with features ready to obey orders.

It also told him to be careful of him.

Andy smiled cheerfully at Stella and nodded politely to Coffin.

'Lady Pinero?'

Stella gave Coffin a quick look. 'Andy... Robert Eglin was a fellow competitor, he was playing beside you in various roles when you tried for your scholarship. ' She didn't wait for the boy to answer. 'You were friends?'

'We were all friends.'

'Of course you were. He was very disappointed not to win?'

'I guess so... but we all knew from the very beginning what a gamble it was.'

'Have you seen him since?'

Andrew said carefully that No, he had not. 'We said good-bye, after the announcement of the winner. He congratulated me and walked away. I haven't seen him since.'

Stella nodded.

'Why don't you ask his girlfriend? They were living and loving together.' There was quiet tartness in his tone that suggested all love should come his way. 'And there was a baby too. He was very disappointed. Of course, anyone would have been. But we all know about the transitory nature of acting success. All except the great greats have their ups and downs.' He smiled radiantly at Stelle Pinero. Not you, of course, the smile said.

'I've had my vissicitudes, I assure you,' said Stella. She turned to Coffin. 'I'll consult the files, see what addresses I can come up with.'

'He's missing, is he?' asked Andrew.

'Sort of.'

'Anyone might, you know. Just hide for a bit.'

And we know where he is, thought Coffin.

Coffin and Stella walked back to her office. 'I'll see what I can find for you to use. Everything may have been destroyed. I ordered them not to keep much.'

'So it will all have gone.' He was gloomy, that was police life on occasion: no one helped you.

Stella laughed. 'No, my team are not speedy movers in office matters... lifting the curtain, performing, yes. We may get something.'

She made a brisk telephone call which soon resulted in the appearance of an apologetic assistant holding out a flat, blue cardboard file.

'There is this, Lady Pinero... empty really.' As she held it out a piece of paper fluttered out. 'That must have got left... just his last address. '

Robert Eglin, 3, Trafalgar Place, off Nelson Street.

'That'll do for a start,' said Coffin reaching out.

It would have to be Phoebe Astley since Les Henderson and Winnie Ardet had assistants answering their phones with the promise to ring back, and Mercy remained elusive.

Chapter 14

'Nelson and Trafalgar,' said Phoebe Astley aloud, as she parked her car at the corner of the two streets. 'They've always been keen on Nelson round here.' She had a young WDC with her, always a wise rule on a house call. 'Not because they disliked the French, but because it upset shipping and shipping was what this part of London depended on. Docks, and ships and cargoes.'

'Not now though,' said the WDC.

'No, not now. Then, it was part of the world's biggest port. Now it's got Heathrow. I don't know if it's the worlds' biggest airport, but it must be near it.'

Phoebe was sensitive about sounds and the constant throb and drum of the planes going into Heathrow irritated her. There was also another airfield further down the river so she got it both ways.

'You have heard of Nelson and Trafalgar, I suppose? You don't think it's to celebrate a football team?'

'No, of course not. ' Her young DC was indignant. 'And Lady Hamilton. I saw the film. Laurence Olivier was Nelson. '

History might not be exactly like that film, thought Phoebe, but why worry.

'Of course, it was an old film,' said the DC.

Three, Trafalgar Place was one of a terrace of thin, tall houses, clearly let out as rooms, with nothing smart about it. It looked clean but cheap.

'Ring the bell and get us in,' she ordered the DC. 'Oh, all right, if the bell won't work bang on the knocker.'

The knocker did work so that soon a cross woman appeared. 'Come in, come in, what is it you want? There's one room to let but I want references and money in advance.' She had the grim determined look of one who knows she isn't going to get a reference (which would be no good anyway)

but is absolutely determined to get the money. 'And more if you two share.'

She thinks we're a pair of lesbians, decided Phoebe.

Once that confusion was cleared up and Phoebe had asked about Robert Eglin, there was some progress. That is, after the woman had managed to remember who Robert was.

She consulted a large red notebook. 'Eglin... don't think that was his real name, he was an actor, or said he was. Probably Potts or Brown.'

Phoebe sighed. One step forward and one back.

'He's been gone a long time. He went off with that poor little creature who lived with him, and the baby. He looked like death.'

'Did he?' She might have been nearer the truth than she knew.

'Paid up, though. Didn't leave owing.'

This was the trio of dead people, Phoebe knew this, but who they really, what their story was, was something else.

Police methods would identify them in the end, she was sure of that, but it would take time. Coffin was not willing to wait.

He might have to, though.

We know who the lad is, we know of his relationship with the girl, and we can guess the child belonged to both of them.

Beyond that, what do we know?

They must have family, they didn't spring from Zeus's forehead.

'Dangerous things, families,' said Coffin, when Phoebe said this to him. 'Never had much of a one myself till Stella took me on.'

Or else he had too much. Abandoned by his mother as a infant, he had been brought up by a 'relation' who turned out to be no relation at all, but his mother's dresser... they had loved each other very much.

Then later, after his own unsuccessful marriage and the

death of a son, he had discovered that mother had survived and married several times. Sensibly to rich men.

Very wise of her, Coffin had said to himself. I might have done the same. But although it was all right for women to look for a rich husband, indeed it was almost expected of them, there was a prejudice about a man marrying for money.

He'd married Stella who could spend money faster than she could earn it, but whom he loved.

Or, as he sometimes suspected, Stella had married him and all he had to do was to say Yes. As Stella had once observed: 'It's such a comfort being married to a top policeman if you are trying to run a theatre, it irons out so many little problems.'

Coffin had been left with a stiff, lawyer half-brother in Edinburgh (his father probably a Scottish Law Lord), and a delicious American half-sister called Laetitia Bingham who was a banker, very rich, but occasionally bankrupt.

The stuffy half-brother was now keeping his distance on account of the serial murders, but Letty had sent an email to say she was coming over and this murder saga *must* make a film. Stella was to see it did. They could use dummies for the dead ladies. At which Coffin winced.

'My family is all right,' said Phoebe to him. 'My sister and her kids.' Not that she wanted kids herself, but she liked her sisters'. Family life at secondhand was probably safest for a police officer.

'So what have we got?' Coffin ignored Phoebe's family reminiscences: he knew she quarrelled with her sister if they were together for longer than a day. 'All we have is his name. If it was his name,'

'Yes, probably his stage name, and his real name was Fisher or Brown.'

'Look it up in THEATRE BOOK, all names and variations are there.'

'I have done. Nothing. Or nothing I could get a handle on.'

Coffin frowned. He never looked disagreeable when he frowned, just thin, thoughtful and anxious.

'I could positively like him when he looks like that,' thought Phoebe. ' But I won't because it would be dangerous. ' Aloud, she said: 'Superintendent Miller has called another meeting of all for us investigating the serial killings, tomorrow morning, 9am sharp.' Since she had started working on the paedophile case, murders and investigations had clustered around her. Not that she'd got far. 'And I think he's asked Joe Jones if he feels up to it.'

'He called it because I told him to... Stella will be there.'

Phoebe let her surprise show.

'She's going to see photographs of all the dead women to see if she knew them.'

Brave of her, thought Phoebe, she won't enjoy it. Then she saw from the expression Coffin's face that Stella had not volunteered, but had been ordered to attend.

Not all bliss being the Chief Commander's wife.

When she got back to work Mercy had both an email and a telephone message telling her of the big meeting so she knew it was serious. She also got one from Phoebe Astley complaining she was hard to track down. She returned to her office, sending an email back to Phoebe Astley. 'Migraine, migraine,' she said in apology, 'you know how it is, you just want to be on your own. Brain pain.'

Brain pain. 'Who wants a hot brain?' she asked herself, 'but sometimes you just get it.' The serial murders of women had done this for her. Superintendent Miller had added to it by sending out the invitation to a big meeting, but she guessed that John Coffin was behind it.

Mercy tried once more to get in touch with Joe. As usual Inspector Joe Jones, who always sheltered behind his wife on the telephone, let Josie speak first. She admitted she had had some time off from the hospital but was on her way back to work.

'And how's Joe?'

'He can talk to you himself.'

He started at once, so Mercy guessed he had been listening to the telephone call. Any good detective would. And Joe was a very good detective but with a style all his own. He had trained young Mercy so she respected it.

'I heard about the bodies that were found. So I knew to be ready for a call in.'

Josie called out; 'Remember to take your tablets with you.'

'Take no notice of her,' said Joe, a sardonic humour in his voice. 'She thinks I might drop dead.'

'It's working in a hospital,' said Mercy. 'Do it to me, I expect.' Her doctor friend was a bit strange sometimes. Stress. She had been worried over Joe herself but was not about to say so.

'Oh a casualty of life,' said Joe. 'How 's Dr Whatever-he's-called?'

Mercy avoided the question. That was a subject to steer clear of.

'I wish I found it easier to work with the Chief Commander, but I don't. Everyone likes him, I like him myself, but I find him hard to work with. Perhaps hard isn't the word, but I feel he expects more than I deliver.' This was about the third meeting that had been called in which they were told how all the recent murders were linked. Were they? And if so, how? Nothing seemed to fit.

'He is a clever man,' said Joe.

'So are you, Joe and you're OK to work with.'

'You know what this summons to a meeting means? The boss is taking over.'

Distantly, through the telephone line, Mercy heard Josie saying; if Lady Pinero's going to be there, then I ought to be too.

'Why?' asked Mercy.

'Because I work in the University Hospital... I see lots of faces. I might recognise one or two.' Josephine sounded emphatic.

'*Lady* Coffin or *Miss* Pinero,' said Joe, he put the receiver down with a clink.

The meeting was held in a large room in an old part of the police building. Stories said that this area had been a school and the big room had been the school hall. On this morning it had had a brush up and polish which a first arrival claimed was for the benefit of the Chief Commander. If Coffin had heard the rumour about the school he would have been able to deny it: he had seen the room when he first took on his job and it was full of old police uniforms and boots with not a smell of food. Besides, there was no kitchen. No kitchen, no food.

He was punctual as were all the summoned detectives. Phoebe Astley was sitting next to Winnie Ardet while Sergeant Les Henderson had tucked himself away behind them. Winnie Ardet was a good-sized girl and he didn't want to be noticed. He had tried to tone down his bright red hair with cream which partly succeeded in flattening it down while not touching the colour. He enjoyed coming to these meetings although had they helped? Yes, probably, at least you could talk things over with your colleagues.

Les looked around at the people who had been working on these serial killings and he was bound to say that they all looked tired and anxious which was how he felt. Everyone had been advised by Miller, always a perfectionist, to bring a short precis of their thoughts and conclusions so they would be fluent and well briefed in case they wanted speak out. Les had his in a blue folder on his knees.

Inspector Joe Jones who had been away ill now looked better than any of them. Les grinned at him and got a grin in return.

On a big screen in front of them, pictures of the murdered women were appearing.

Amy Buckly, with her long hair, falling across her face. An early photograph, Les decided, taken as soon as the police photographer got there. Nothing of the morgue about it. She had not been tidied up.

Mary Rice. Spectacles pushed away. Yes, that had been a nasty one. Not one that he had been working on himself, but he had gone to see the body in case it helped with Phillida Jessup.

Yes, there was Phillida on the screen. Really chewed up, poor Phillida. She had been one of the cases he had concentrated on which had not been easy. Nor successful, he had got nowhere.

Angela Dover. Had they called her Angela or Angie when she was alive? He had gone to the inquest on Angela, then he had been diverted back to work on Phillida. He had had the mournful feeling that he would have liked Angela if he had seen her alive. She wasn't that young, but then neither was he, but maybe in a different time or place they could have gone a long way together. Sometimes he felt this way about cases he was involved in.

Finally, the last body, so far. Must remember to say that because there could be another any minute. Lotty Brister was older than the other girls although she could have been younger, her body discovered in Peppard Alley, thrown into the gutter, almost as if she had been a mistake. In the working clothes for her elegant shop - Prada suit, Wolford tights - she had looked extremely youthful.

There was little comment as the pictures came up and settled into position on the screen. The audience watched in virtual silence. It meant that there was hardly any progress. This show would not be put on if the police had a suspect.

'Clever chap, this killer,' murmured Phoebe. 'Curse him.'

'We'll get him in the end,' said Winnie Ardet.

'Think so?' Disillusionment was starting to show.

Winnie did not answer.

'No, you don't really think so,' said Phoebe.

'In time. Give us time, we'll get there in the end.'

Phoebe shook her head. 'I feel as though he's watching us, this chap.'

'Have you had this feeling with other murders?' asked Winnie.

Phoebe shook her head. 'No.'

'I have. Once, and in fact that killer *was* watching me. But he was caught.'

There was a pause, then Phoebe said: 'You don't think he could be a doctor, do you?' Phoebe knew that Mercy was having a tough time with doctors at the moment. But she kept silent.

All the pictures of the victims were now lined up on the screen.

'My wife has looked at all these faces,' said John Coffin. 'And she is sure that she knows several of them. She feels it is most likely that she saw them in one of the theatres.'

A voice called out: 'Performers?'

Stella put her head down and did not answer. Coffin did so for her.

'No, she thinks not, but she feels she saw the victims in or around the theatre. '

'Does this mean the killer is...' the speaker fumbled for words '...close to the theatre?'

Coffin shrugged. He did not answer.

Superintendent Miller intervened with the sort of bland no-answer response that could madden his colleagues.

'All the teams are, of course, going into the background of the victims. Lady Coffin's help will not be forgotten.'

Inspector Ardet muttered audibly; 'As if we haven't been doing that already.'

And this is where the Chief Commander ought to admit that he is going to do a lot of it himself, was the Superintendent's quiet internal comment. He was one of those who, while admiring John Coffin's skill as a detective, could not help resisting or resenting his equal skill at inserting himself into an investigation. Miller felt that circumstances somehow helped him into it.

In as commanding a voice as he could manage, not easy with both the Chief Commander and Stella Pinero present, Miller asked if anyone had anything further to say.

There was a short silence. Then Les Henderson stood up. 'Sergeant Henderson, sir. I think we can make a good guess at the age and workings of the killer.

'He is not a young person. Middle-aged.

'He has help.'

There was still silence.

'All right: it may not seem much, but I think it is: I reckon we have a shape and an age and a *companion*. That is something.'

Five homes to visit, five mourning families to talk with. The investigating teams thought about this as they filed out.

There had been some discussion about Les's description of the killer. To his surprise, it was accepted by most of those who spoke. Yes, it seemed reasonable that the killer was a middle-aged man with a helper. 'Not a youngster's crime,' one officer said. 'Too bloody organised,' was another comment. 'All have the same sort of look, those women... I don't know what it is, but it's there. It's why they were chosen.'

'It's because they're dead,' said one cynic, 'and because we know they were chosen.'

The Chief Commander heard this floating on the air as the cynic marched out.

'Good comment. But no future in acting on it.'

Coffin and Stella were the last to leave in company with Superintendent Miller.

'That do any good, do you think, sir?'

'Might have stirred up some ideas. All the women, except possibly the last victim, looked as if they came from the same sort of background.'

'Middle class, you mean, sir.' The Superintendent was well

known to be a man of highly conservative views although surprisingly he always voted Labour.

'I suppose I do.' Coffin added: 'Bit of background's useful sometimes, I think, don't you?' It wasn't quite a question but Miller knew he had to give the right answer.

'I suppose it is.' He added: 'Sir' after a pause.

'You had a look at the homes and houses, I suppose.'

'Only the victim I was working on, sir.'

Stella knew her place on most occasions. This was one in which to keep quiet. In fact, she wanted to get back to the theatre. Sometimes John seemed to think the theatres, all three of them, ran themselves. Far from the truth. There was a minor crisis on at the moment as the news got around about the three dead bodies. For herself, she had been more disturbed by the deaths than she found it easy to admit.

This mood had been deepened by an excited and emotional call from her sister-in-law, Laeticia Bingham. Letty was coming to the Second City. Expect her, was the message.

She looked at her husband whom she had not yet told of the impending arrival of his explosively powerful sister. She thought when he found out he would not be best pleased.

'I'd like to take a look around myself,' he was saying.

Oh yes, thought Miller, saw that coming. You want in, Sir John? Well, you're welcome. 'Do you want me to come with you, sir?'

'A couple of men, do you think?' Coffin was thoughtful.

'Taking a woman officer with you, might be wiser,' volunteered the Super.

You always jump the way he wants, he thought, and that must be why he has the position he has and you are where you are.

'Chief Inspector Phoebe Astley might be a good choice.'

But before John Coffin had a chance to do anything, another woman came onto the scene.

She was not alive. Nor, for that matter, was she dead. She

had never been alive. She was the model woman that had been deposited in no very friendly way in the tower of St Luke's. She was not exactly a murder victim herself but she was a preamble to, an announcement of, violence. She was hate personified.

Or that was how she had seemed to John Coffin.

Her origin, who had bought her, for she was not a woman who had come free, had not been discovered.

But DC Peter Gittings, young and eager, had now found out where she came from and been eager to pass on the news.

Direct access to the Chief Commander himself was, of course, denied him, but he got as close as he could by telling Paul Masters. He was sitting in the canteen, drinking a big cup of coffee with milk and biting on a hot bacon sandwich, considering the good luck that had fallen upon him, when Paul took the only seat in the room which was next to Peter.

A friendly soul and never one to stand on ceremony, Paul said he could quite fancy a bacon sandwich himself now he smelt that one. He was rewarded (if that was what it was) by the prompt appearance of one accompanied by Peter's triumphant saga.

'Chief Inspector Astley told me to find out where the dummy came from and get a description of the buyer if I could. I tried everywhere: sport shops, dress shops, health outfits, sex shops,' a delicate pink blush spread over his youthful cheeks. 'No go.'

'So?' Paul swallowed his mouthful of bacon butty which he was enjoying more than he had expected because he had already had a full breakfast. He'd have to buy a lad a drink or another bacon sandwich, couldn't sponge off him.

'Well, I hadn't much to go on, you see... just a rough guess at the date it might have been bought and that it was probably a man buying. Then I remembered the little junk shop in Ship Street... they sell everything there... it's quite respectable...' There was a faint note of doubt in his voice.

Not so very respectable then, thought Paul.

'And they had sold one. Within the right period, the right type. They showed me one like it... back up stock, I suppose. But...' and his eyes went wide, 'they sold it to a *woman.'* Paul Masters thought about it. 'Did she take it with her? Naked or wrapped up?'

'The assistant packaged it up. Not the first one she'd sold, she knew what to do. But it was bulky and heavy.'

'How did the woman manage?'

'She managed all right, she was a big woman and she had a car waiting for her, or so the assistant thought. It's not the sort of shop where you ask questions or rush out to give a hand to the customer.'

'Would she know the woman again?'

Peter shrugged, a little of his confidence falling away. 'She says she thinks she might; But it's if we find the woman first. Can't go combing the streets of London for all women nearly six feet tall.'

'Is that the description?'

Peter nodded. 'I wish I could add more.' His bacon butty was beginning to weigh heavily in his stomach. 'I'll keep my eyes open...'

'I think you've done well. You've put your report in? Good, I'll see the Chief Commander knows.' He stood up.

'Oh thank you, sir.'

Peter felt so happy that he was hungry again. He went up to the counter to order another bacon sandwich.

'What, another one?' said Edith, the girl on duty, a bonny creature whom Peter secretly fancied. Perhaps not so secretly from the smile she always gave him. 'That's three.'

'Only two for me.'

'Have to give you an extra bit of sauce then.'

He grinned. 'Like always?'

'Cheeky you.'

He dropped his grin and became serious. 'I could get tickets for this Saturday then at the Palladium... if you'd like to come.'

She looked thoughtful.

'See you home, of course.'

'Well...'

'And meet you to take you there... can't be too careful.'

'No, right. You're on.'

John Coffin got the news about the model from Paul Masters very promptly. He knew the shop too.

'See the news gets to the Incident Room.'

'Have done, sir.'

'Not that it's worth much.' Coffin was thoughtful. 'Not on its own. Need a bit more detail... In fact, all the details.'

Paul grinned. 'Pete Gittings is a good lad, but he needs a bit more experience in winkling things out of witnesses. Usually the crucial things. That which they wish to hide.'

'Dare I suggest you go yourself and take a look round?'

'Well, sir, it's really part of Phoebe Astley's case but we could settle it between us, I guess.' In fact, there was no guessing, he knew already, such was the speed with which information about their colleagues passed around HQ that Phoebe Astley was due to do some work with the Chief. Did he mind? A little, he had always worked closely with the Chief while Phoebe moved around.

But it didn't matter, he had his own ambitions and was marking a path out according to them. Keeping on good terms with John Coffin was certainly part of it, but not working with him forever, much as he liked the man. As he did. Impossible not to.

'Actually I might look in myself.' Coffin considered. 'I knew the proprietor in my younger South London days. I was surprised when the splendid old cockney turned up here.'

'We're all cockney's here, sir.' Masters spoke with the polite amusement of ex-Public school and Oxford.

'So we are.' Coffin knew he was by ancestry and upbringing but life (and Stella) had put a gloss on him. His musings were interrupted by a telephone call from Stella herself.

'This is just to tell you that Letty is flying in today. Heathrow this evening.'

His beloved but somewhat feared sister. Coffin groaned. 'Is she staying with us?'

'No, Claridges, says she doesn't want to be any trouble. '

'She will be though, she always is.'

Stella laughed. 'She says she's coming over to help you with this murder business... I think she probably plans a film or TV show.'

Coffin groaned again.

'And she hopes we will recognise her, she's had facial surgery. And this trip to us is her treat for being a good patient.'

'Oh God.'

'She'll look lovely, never fear. She'll have gone to the best cosmetic surgeon in New York.'

'I hope you'll never do the same.'

What I do with my face is my own business, thought Stella. 'Don't suppose I'll ever have the money.' Then she added thoughtfully, 'Although, of course, as a performer it would be tax deductable... I must speak to my accountant.'

'Now I know you're joking.'

Over the telephone line, he heard the sound of barking.

'You've got Gus with you.'

'I wanted company.'

'Would you like to come shopping with me?'

'If it's the sort of shopping I think it is, then the answer is no.'

Coffin laughed, but gently. 'You can read my mind. I suppose it's why I love you.'

'Not all husbands would feel the same. ' Her voice softened. 'Don't get into trouble, my love, will you?'

'Certainly not. Why should I?'

'Because it's the way you operate. It's known as sailing close to the wind.'

'Not me, never.' But he knew he did, especially if as now, Stella was involved. As she was, somehow. How and why, he did not know, but by God, he would find out.

'Look after yourself,' Stella said, no laughter now in her voice.

'You do the same.'

'You've given me a minder again, haven't you? Don't think I haven't noticed.'

Coffin kept silent. But not for long: 'I won't go on my own. Phoebe Astley will be with me.'

But this was a lie. He was going alone. He knew the owner and eminence gris of the shop in question, remembered him from the old days in Deptford, recalled enough to know that he would never talk in front of a third party, let alone a woman. With Coffin on his own he might let something interesting out.

Wearing carefully chosen, unobtrusive clothes, Coffin strolled into the shop, pushing aside a large stuffed cat, several boxes full of what looked like old clothes, and a big, old-fashioned, crocodile skin trunk (which he tripped against, causing a confused noise), to be greeted by his old acquaintance. You couldn't say friend, since Coffin had been active in sending him to prison once, if not twice, years ago. As far as he knew, though, there had been no reason for imprisonment since the move to the Second City.

'Hello, Johnny boy. Long time no see... 'course, I knew you were in the Second City, top of the heap too.'

'Not quite,' said Coffin, rubbing his ankle.

'Lovely object, isn't it? Can't you just imagine it, travelling on the old Queen Mary to New York, or being put on the train in Paris by your maidservant to go to the South of France while you chatted to Noel Coward.'

'I didn't know you were such a romantic, Bert,' said Coffin, still rubbing his ankle.

'At heart, Johnny, at heart. Always was. Not a side of me you saw, Johnny.'

'No, it wasn't.' Prison for fraud, then robbery with some violence - a girlfriend with a badly fractured cheekbone did not readily call up a picture of a romantic man.

'I kept it hidden. Had to, you know what it was like living in John Evelyn Street.' Bert smiled radiantly. 'But now it can come out.'

'That must be nice for you.'

'Better than you think... look around and see what I've collected, some things to keep forever, like the trunk, and others to sell.'

'Like the model of a naked woman.'

There was moment of silence.

'Ah.' Bert did not cease to smile but perhaps his eyes hardened. 'I knew you didn't come in just to say Hello and How are you.'

'You sold a model recently. I need to know more about the sale: to whom, for instance?'

'We always keep a modest stock of these ladies, not always on show, but those who want one know where to come. Sometimes they are needed for...' he coughed tactfully, '... for medical reasons, sometimes for artistic reasons...' He gave up at this point and was silent.

Coffin waited in silence.

'That lady was one of my favourites, she'd been with us for some time and I'd got to like her. You might think there's no difference between one and another, but there is if you live with them long enough.'

'All right,' said Coffin impatiently, 'after you have lived long enough with one of these models to get attached to her, then you *do* sell it. It is a matter of business, after all.'

'Well, yes, Johnny, yes, a profit must come. We insist on cash.'

'Yes, yes, so I daresay you know most of your customers?'

'Not by name.' said Bert with decision. 'Couldn't expect it. I didn't sell the model, I might not have let her go, I like to think of them going to a good home. Like a dog, you know. My wife sold her.'

'I'd like to speak to her.'

Bert nodded. He went to the back door to shout. 'Myrtle, Myrtle. Here with you.'

A memory stirred inside Coffin. Myrtle? Surely that had been the name of the very young and pretty girl whose cheek-bone had been cracked? They'd married, had they? What a courtship.

In through the door came one of the thinnest women that Coffin had ever seen, so tall that she had to bend her head to get through the door.

'Ah, there you are, Mirt.'

Mirt, Myrtle... this was what the slender, pretty girl had turned into: a figure of length and no breadth with the pretty features pointed and sharp. A bit bruised as well, so Bert had not changed.

'This copper wants to ask you about the dummy you sold.'

Mirt did not recognise him.

'Who did you sell it to?'

She shrugged. 'Some tall thin bird in trousers.'

'Lesbian?' asked Bert. He sounded unsurprised.

She shrugged again. 'Could be.'

Bert looked at Coffin: 'We get birds going both ways. You should see some of them. Some don't even know for sure themselves.'

'Would you know her again?' asked Coffin.

Mirt shook her head. 'Doubt it.'

'Why are you so worried?' asked Bert.

Coffin did not answer. What could he say? That it was left as a present for my wife and I wouldn't mind killing whoever it was?

'Wait a minute,' said Myrtle. ' I remember you now: you're John Coffin, and you're a big boss figure now. You arrested my Bert once.'

'He deserved it.'

'Course he did. And more.'

'Here,' protested Bert.

His wife ignored him, while she studied Coffin's face. What she saw there seemed to interest her.

'These questions you're asking. Got anything to do with all these murders?'

'Why? What makes you say that?' said Coffin alertly. For the first time he saw that there was a sharp, observant face imbedded in that flesh and bone.

There was a moment when no one spoke. Coffin waited, determined not to be the first to break the silence.

'I don't know,' said Myrtle. 'It's just the sort of thing you coppers do.'

'Is that all?'

She walked towards the back door. At the door, she said vaguely over her shoulder, as if she might mean something or she might not, just talking. 'Oh don't know. Just if I saw him-her walking around the Second City, then I might give you a ring.'

Chapter 15

Phoebe told Joe Jones and Sergeant Les Henderson, both of whom were having drinks with her, that tomorrow she was going round the houses where each victim had lived with the Chief Commander.

'We know that,' said Les.

'And it behoves me to look out for myself. '

'I thought you liked him.'

'I do, he's a great man, I've known him a long while, and worked with him, but you have to watch yourself with his lordship, he is tough.'

They were drinking in the Golden Fleece, a bar popular with the Second City CID. It was early evening so the place was not crowded.

'You're nervous,' said Les, surprised. She's in love with him, he thought, or she was once. Is now, said a realistic voice inside him. He's a bloody attractive man, damn him. Les had always fancied Phoebe himself. Not in love with her, he wasn't ready for a big emotion like that, but one or two pegs short of it, maybe.

'Never seen Phoebe nervous,' said Joe.

`Not nervous, just anxious,' Phoebe replied quickly.

'Keep us in touch, tell us everything and Les and I will help, won't we, Les?' Joe offered with a grin.

Les had worked with both Joe and Phoebe in his time and he thought that Phoebe was the one who saw further into the wood. 'Maybe,' he said.

'Oh come on,' said Phoebe. 'I'm not buying you a drink to make me miserable but to cheer me up.'

Joe was a good detective but not one it was easy to find relaxing, not "jollity country" as Les had put it once. But he had somehow joined the party with Les. Les was a friend, Phoebe suspected it was because he reminded her of a much younger John Coffin, but better perhaps not to go into that.

'I'm just a sort of chaperone, going round the homes, a woman better than a man.'

'Interesting thought,' said Les. 'I wish he'd asked me.'

'Oh it had to be a woman... expendable when not needed,' said Phoebe with some bitterness.

'You don't believe that,' said Les.

'No, perhaps not. Anyway, we start tomorrow. His lordship could not manage earlier, an important meeting in London... the other London, the bigger and richer one.'

'I think you are just very slightly drunk,' said Les kindly.

'Never.'

Phoebe had received a telephone call from Paul Masters setting out the arrangements late that afternoon while working on records in her new office. She had been on her own and with an aching head. No doubt, as a later sober reflection would point out to her, this had added to the irritation that Paul Masters had told her what she was to do and not the Chief Commander himself.

'I suppose they've already had the forensic teams round there?' she had enquired.

'Oh yes.' Cheerfully, Masters added: 'I'll see you get them all.'

'Reckon I've got them,' she looked at her overburdened desk. She knew as Masters did that reports surged in on investigations such as this one and were read quickly. Then sometimes forgotten. There was only just so much you could take in, retain and use. This was the weakness of criminal investigations: you needed a polyheaded detective.

She had read them, though, and had now packed them away to take home to read again. Just in case. She knew from experience how sharp Coffin was on detail.

'Better get home,' she said now to Les and Joe. 'Early start tomorrow.'

'She won't solve the murders,' said Joe, watching her go. 'Not in that mood.'

'Oh I don't know. She's good. And she'll have the Chief with her and he can be more than good.'

Joe shrugged. 'He's had luck, I grant you that.'

'He's got talent... look at his history. Came up from nothing, mother left him behind and moved on...' He paused as he knew enough about Coffin to know that his mother had moved on to fresher and more profitable fields. Coffin must, in some ways, be like his mother.

Joe smiled, he had a good smile, Les thought, but with hidden mirth behind it. He must get to know him better and find out what the mirth was about. All detective work should start at home. His motto.

Phoebe waved at them from the door, Les waved back. 'Good luck, girl.'

'So you think she needs it?' Joe probed.

'Everyone does, don't they? Now and again, or all the time some cases. Like another drink?'

'I'll get them. My shout.'

Les watched him return carrying two glasses. 'Glad to see you back, Joe. It was rotten luck being ill. Are you feeling up to it?'

'Oh yes, sure. Bit of a false alarm I'm glad to say. But when you have a wife who's a power in the local hospital, you tend to get taken seriously when you fancy any symptoms.'

Les gave a laugh. 'I wouldn't call you the imaginative sort, Joe.'

'Everyone can be on occasion... even *my* wife. You married?'

'No,' Les managed to sound regretful although a spouse would have severely cut into his love life. 'Those I fancied didn't seem to fancy me. I will marry hopefully. I'd like a kid. You got any?'

'Stepson.'

'You can love him just as much.'

'Sure.' Joe finished his drink, and stood up. 'Better get home.'

Les had one more drink and a sandwich before departing himself. He lived in a small flat on the ground floor of a block in Spinnergate. Contrary to what might have been expected of him as a male officer in the CID, he kept it immaculate. The bed was made before he left for work, the breakfast dishes washed and dried, the furniture was dusted and sometimes polished - but that was because he liked the smell of the polish. He even ironed his own shirts. He had one black cat who had befriended him but who knew to keep the rules: home early, stay in at night, and don't bring in a mouse. (Or if you must, don't let master see.)

He had asked Phoebe Astley round for a drink once and seen her looking at the polished wood and concluding he had a cleaner to do the work. He had been in her flat once too and knew that not only did she not have a help but did very little herself. His housewifely fingers had itched to dust a rather good table she had.

Phoebe had noticed the dust but the table had still remained unpolished as she walked in that evening. She opened her bag and tipped out the papers she needed to work on. She wished she knew what Coffin would be looking out for as they went round where the victims lived.

She fell asleep with the papers all around her, then woke up, to shower, drink some coffee and drive to the station.

Coffin was ready for her. 'Stella wanted to come on this tour with me,' he said cheerfully.

Phoebe was startled. 'Why?' She could not believe that Stella wearing casual (but couture) clothes would be a fit figure to go on this particular trail. Up stairs and down stairs, in and out, and probably without point in the end.

'I think because she felt she was an early victim but one that got away.'

A nasty feeling, thought Phoebe, could be true as well. 'Did she want to come instead of me or as well as?' she asked.

'She didn't make that clear. As well as, I expect.'

'I wouldn't have minded,' Phoebe said. 'She would have

added her own way of looking at things. Might have been valuable.'

Coffin did not answer. The truth was that he did not want Stella more mixed up with this affair than she already was.

'It's a task for the professional,' was all he said. And then: 'I'll drive.'

It was going to be a quiet, gentle entrance, not the police cars and supporters the Chief could command - and did so, when it suited him.

They would know him, of course. More people knew him than Coffin realised. He'd have to identify himself officially anyway. Phoebe might remain anonymous.

'What excuse do we use for coming?' After all, each household had already been interviewed and inspected.

'Do we need one?' Coffin was negotiating the difficult exit from the parking lot. It was always crowded and desperate souls sneaked in where and how they could.

'No, I suppose not. Not with you in charge, sir.'

Coffin drove on silently at speed.

'Where do we start, sir?'

'With the first victim: Amy Buckly.'

Coffin knew where he was going through the network of narrow streets. They had been constructed by a Victorian builder, solid enough to survive two great wars with two air bombardments, after economic depression and the departure of the big ships from the dock. But now the little houses were bright with paint and small front gardens full of roses and window boxes jolly with geraniums. A smart car was as likely to be jostling for parking along the kerb as once the motorbike might have been. It was the new prosperity, born not of manual labour but expertise in the new technologies. The inhabitants of the docklands had always been open-minded and quick learners and now could do business with their emails with the best. This vitality had brought them through Tudor prosperity, Stuart civil wars, Hanoverian naval wars and

Victorian imperial power. Now the residents could be seen trotting up and down the streets, some still cobbled, ears tight to mobile phones.

The smartness was patchy however, some areas acheiving the look before others, but where Amy Buckly had lived was one of the richer streets. A well-dressed man in a silk shirt and a tie of flowing beauty that almost matched his hair was walking past the car as they drove up. He did not look up from his mobile at first but as they edged into a clear spot by the kerb space, he took notice.

'Hey, that's my parking space.'

Coffin leaned out of the window. 'Police.'

'Oh yes, easy to say that.'

Coffin nodded at Phoebe who produced her card.

'Fuck you,' said the telephone holder, still managing to continue his conversation. 'No, not you, Debby, at least not right now,' he added wickedly.

Coffin got out of the car, locking it behind him and went up to the door of the house.

'I don't think there will be anyone there, unless her family has moved back in. They left after the murder. Couldn't stand it.' Phoebe was feeling in her pocket. 'I've got a key.'

'Who took over the case?'

'Superintendent Miller. He gave me the key.'

There was a shrill barking from behind the door.

'Someone's back.'

'Yes, she had a dog.'

The door was opened by a tall, pretty young woman. She seemed unsurprised to see them and held the door open wider in a tacit invitation to enter.

'Let me see now, Sergeant Henderson assisted,' said Coffin thoughtfully.

'I knew you were coming.' She was eyeing Phoebe. 'Chief Inspector Astley?'

Coffin gave Phoebe a speculative look. So Les Henderson was not the gossip.

Phoebe could see what he was thinking, she hastened to defend herself.

'No, not through me.And I don't think I know you, Miss Buckly.'

'No, but I saw you when you came to the school, Close Street school, about a paedophile case you were working on a year or so ago. You didn't speak to me nor to Amy as far as I know but of course, we knew who you were.' The dog was winding itself round her feet but keeping a sharp gaze on the two visitors.

'One of the kids was a victim. Dragged into a van and kept overnight, then dumped.' She stared directly at Phoebe, 'We were all very upset.'

'We're still working on it,' said Phoebe hastily. Although Heaven knew she hadn't done much lately. The small boy, Victor Passy, as she remembered, had been a poignantly painful case to investigate, brutal indeed, but the interesting thing was that as even she had talked to him, she had seen that he was a resilient kid and was recovering well. 'We often have to work on more than one case at once.'

There was silence, the girl said thoughtfully: 'Are you saying that the paedophile cases and the murders are connected?'

Coffin answered for them both: 'No, we don't think so.' The girl said: 'Yes, I see what you mean: the sort of person who would get sexual pleasure from abusing a child would probably not get it from killing an adult. And the other way round.'

She picked up the dog which licked her cheek. 'I hope you are right, and telling me the truth.'

Coffin nodded. 'Yes.' This was a clever, shrewd girl, not one you lied to. He felt cold dip inside him: he knew that he had not paid enough attention to the paedophile cases because of Stella and the murders. 'I'm not on speakers with this rotten case,' he said inside, 'and I mustn't blame Stella.'

'I'm glad because I'd been wondering if Amy's murder was because she knew Victor. He was in her class.' Her big blue eyes studied them. 'See what I mean.' She patted the dog's head so that he rolled round to look her in the face.

'Was he a boy you taught too?'

'I'm not a teacher... I work in the office. She was Amy, Amabel really but she preferred it short. I'm Deborah.'

Coffin knew where he had to go.

'Deborah, may we take a look at Amy's room?'

The girl looked away, then down at her hands.

'We won't disturb anything.'

She still said nothing. Coffin had the feeling that unless he kept the conversation going she would disappear.

'You lived together, didn't you, Deborah? You shared the house?'

Deborah nodded. Still wordlessly.

'I promise you we will be careful... we won't disturb anything. Come with us to watch.'

He had got through at last.

'You don't understand... I haven't been in her room since she died. I couldn't. ' Phoebe said something under breath. 'No, truly... I took the two detectives to the door when they came but I stood outside, I didn't go in... I think they photographed everything... some things they took away... I was told what, but I tried not to listen. When they went, I locked the door and I haven't been back. I suppose it seems mad to you.'

'No, not mad,' Coffin protested gently. He looked at Phoebe.

'It was sensible,' she said at once. 'I might have done the same myself. Do you feel up to going in now?'

Deborah took several deep breaths as she hugged the dog to her, then she nodded. 'I'll unlock the door... let you in.'

'Thank you. If you would.' In fact, Coffin had a key, handed to him by the original investigating team. Just as well that Deborah did not know how much of the house's equipment was stowed away in the box in the Record Room, neatly labelled and ready to be used if necessary. In a neat package were the underclothes that Amy had had on when she was killed. He wondered how Deborah would feel if she knew.

The young woman drew the room key from her pocket. 'I was meaning to open up tonight...' she said in a matter of fact way.

'Good for you.'

It was a pretty house with light flowered curtains at the windows to match the white paint and soft blue walls that ran up the staircase.

'It was time.' He felt she was keeping her tone deliberately dry. 'I might not have managed it... I saw her when she was dead. I had to identify her.'

Phoebe put her arm round the girl's shoulders.

'Better me than anyone else,' said Deborah.

They had arrived at the door at the top of the staircase. Deborah put in the key, slowly turned it, then pushed at the door.

'It smells in here,' she said.

It did. Any room shut up for more than the odd day takes on its own smells. Here it was a mixture of cosmetics, sweet and a bit sickly and feminine scents coming from the clothes flung here and there on the bed and chairs.

'Nothing an open window won't clear,' said Coffin cheerfully. He did not offer to open the window. It was Amy's room still, her presence was strong. 'Do you want to go? I promise you that we will take care.'

'No, I must stay,' I am the protector, her tone said.

Coffin nodded; he accepted this.

The room was tidy in a casual kind of way as if the owner expected to be back to put things in greater order. The bed was made but a dressing gown of pink silk with a matching nightdress lay across the bed ready to be put away.

Coffin heard Deborah draw in her breath as she looked but she did not move forward. Just stood still.

'OK?' queried Phoebe.

Deborah nodded slowly, three times as if in exorcism of what she saw.

On the bed table a line of books stood, they were a catholic collection: Rankin, Reginald Hill, Armistead Maupin, and a clearly much loved and often read copy of *Bleak House*.

'Almost his best book, I've always thought, ' said Coffin, looking at the Dickens.

'Oh, do you think so?' She went over to touch the books with a gentle forefinger.

'For my taste, yes.'

'Better than *David Copperfield*? Amy always said so.'

'I agree.'

For her part, Phoebe was looking at the dressing table on which were tubs of cream for the face, eye make up, lipstick... famous names: Dior, Lancome, Arden. A spray of scent caught her eye: *l'Heure Bleu*, by Guerlain.

'Damn it,' Phoebe said to herself. 'I would have liked this woman, we used the same scent.' She couldn't afford it very often, but when she could, then it was what she bought.

'I like the Guerlain.' she said aloud.

Deborah laughed for the first time. 'Something I didn't agree with Amy on; I'm a flowers girl. Lavender or rose. Simple, eh?' Her voice was stronger. She went over to the window which she threw open.'Amy wouldn't have wanted the window closed forever. And I think I ought to do a bit of dusting.'

'Looks all right to me,' said Phoebe. I'm starting to sound more and more like Les Henderson with his soothing remarks, she told herself.

In fact, the room was dusty, not really dirty, but it looked neglected. And why not? The woman who had slept in this room was dead. Murdered, one of a series of victims.

She knew well what her part was at this moment: it was to keep Deborah diverted from Coffin. He would also, of course, want her intelligent observations on the room, the house and Deborah to add to his own.

What else he was looking for, she did not know.

Then she heard the Chief Commander give a surprised exclamation. 'Stella, that's Stella.'

Behind the row of books on the bed table, propped up against the wall was a photograph. Unframed but placed so that Amy lying in bed could see it.

It was certainly Stella. A theatrical photograph, taken, as Phoebe remembered, when she was acting in a Coward play. She looked lovely. And genuine. Although it was a piece of theatrical publicity for Stella dressed for the part in a wisp of satin and pearls, she looked genuine and honest and free.

A marvellous way to look even if you are acting, thought Phoebe.

'Oh yes,' said Deborah, 'that's Miss Pinero. Amy was such a great admirer of hers. She went to see every play she was in that she could get to. And of course, the theatre here was a great treat to her... I'd forgotten she had that photograph.' She picked it up. 'Goodness, it's lovely, isn't it?'

Coffin agreed fondly it was a beautiful picture. Also, he remembered but did not mention what Stella had said at the time. 'He was a lovely man, don't think I'm saying otherwise, but he said to keep my head as the light was better for me that way... I knew what that meant - sagging, wrinkles...' Coffin had protested that she had no wrinkles and did not sag. Anywhere. But Stella had burned on, temper hot: 'And he said he'd loved me since he was at school. School! You can imagine how old that made me feel. I'm not sure he didn't say nursery school.' Coffin had muttered something soothing. 'Well, possibly not nursery school but school. But he did turn in a lovely photograph.'

Deborah held the photograph to her. 'I must look after this.' She smiled at Coffin. 'I know she is really Lady Coffin but to me, and to Amy, she's Stella Pinero.'

'Thank you,' said Coffin humbly. 'Do you know, she is to me too.'

They did not stay long after that. Deborah seemed glad to see them go. But she was polite.

'Tell me if there is anything I can do, I want to help any way I can... I told the other nice young woman who came so. She understood... I loved my sister.'

'Of course you did.' Coffin hesitated: 'Did Amy...?'

'Yes,' said Deborah. 'I know what you're going to ask me, I've already been asked by your officers, twice at least. Yes, she did have a boyfriend, in fact more than one, but nothing special... I gave Superintendent Miller their names. '

Both the Chief Commander and Phoebe had read the names with addresses and little character assessments. Nothing much, these reports. Deborah was just putting a little flesh on the bare bones.

Coffin was thoughtful and Phoebe quiet as they left the house. The street outside was quiet too. She wanted to say something but she waited until they were in the car.

'Did you get anything that helped?' she asked eventually. 'Did you get what you wanted?'

'I might have done, I'm still thinking about it.'

So I was just padding, thought Phoebe. Didn't matter whether I was there or not. Right, she thought, well, I'm going to give him a bloody big shock.

She reached into her pocket. 'You saw the photograph of Stella that was on the bed table.'

'Go on, what are you leading up to, Phoebe?'

'But you didn't see this one. Neither did Deborah. It was under the pillow. I just saw the edge, I saw it sticking out. I don't think the bed has been touched since Amy rushed out that last morning.' Phoebe handed over what she had to Coffin. 'Deborah didn't see me and I thought you 'd rather she didn't see this.'

Coffin took it. 'Good Lord, ' he said.

Chapter 16

'Good Lord,' said Coffin again. He was looking down at what she had given him. 'Get in the car.'

'Shall I drive, sir?'

'Yes, better maybe.' He moved from behind the wheel. 'Just to the end of the road. Find somewhere quiet then stop. I want to think.' He was looking at a photograph of himself. He couldn't place where he was, but he must have been leaving a meeting. A snapshot really, but taken by whom?

Amy Buckly herself, perhaps. One thing he did know was that he had had no idea it was being taken. This picture, unlike Stella's, which was a posed, studio photograph, was a stolen likeness.

'Good Lord,' he said again. 'I'm repeating myself, I don't usually do that.'

'It's shock.' Phoebe said.

'It certainly is: you don't expect to see your own face looking at you when you are investigating a murder.'

'You weren't surprised to see Stella.'

'She's a public figure.'

'So are you.' But she knew what the rub was.

'This is not a professional photograph,' he said grimly.

Ah, there it was, thought Phoebe. And it was under the girl's pillow too.

'The sister didn't see, and neither did Miller's investigation team.'

'It's evidence, of a sort. Not to be moved.

'Well, sir. You are the chief officer of the Police Force investigating the murder, and I am one of the CID officers working on the case. So I reckon if anyone has a right to remove it, then we have.'

'It must all be recorded, where we found it, when, the lot.' Then he added: 'Damn it.' He was always uncomfortable when evidence was overlooked. How could they have missed this?

'You don't have to tell Stella.'

Coffin allowed himself a small laugh. 'She'll get to know. You know the Second City: breathe a bit of news in one end and it's coming out the other twice as loud by the end of the day.'

'Sooner sometimes, 'agreed Phoebe who had often played her own part in that happy game. 'Stella won't mind about her own photograph. '

'I shall tell her everything in the end.'

'Of course, you will.'

Phoebe had found a quiet spot near a small park. A large green lawnmower with a man sitting on the top was cutting the grass.

'He's making a noise.' Coffin sounded grumpy.

'It's called cutting the grass.' But she made the joke in a subterranean whisper. There had been times in their relationship when you could make jokes about the Chief Commander aloud but at the moment it behoved her to watch her mouth.

'Well, push on, it's Mary Rice's home next... she died ten days after Amy. I wonder what won her that honour.'

'Chance. Bad luck.'

Coffin looked at her soberly, as she negotiated a turn in the road away from the park; she seemed to know where she was going.

'Chance?' Do you really think that? I am beginning to think that there was not much chance about the killings.

The second part of this statement Coffin suppressed inside himself. Without either side knowing it, he and Phoebe were conducting a silent dialogue.

'Well, the victims didn't know it was going to happen to them when they walked down that particular road at that particular time... and the killer just took what was coming to him. That's what I mean by chance.'

'A very vivid exposition of it too, Phoebe. You are lucid. It's one of the things that makes you a good detective. Where are we, by the way, and where are we going?'

'Tennyson Street, sir. That's the address.'

'After the poet, unless he was the local builder.'

'No, round the corner is Dickens Road and Shakespeare Street next to that. It's a literary district.'

Tennyson Street was a terrace of late Victorian houses which had been badly bombed, then rebuilt so they were now no period at all, but they looked comfortable and well cared for.

'She had a flat here, top floor, but she worked in inner London. I called here myself just after the killing.'

'I thought you knew the way.' Coffin was staring up at the plain faced brick house. 'She lived alone? Or so the notes said.'

Phoebe nodded. 'Most of the time. The odd boyfriend. No one there when she died.'

'There's someone there now. I saw a curtain move.'

Coffin rang the doorbell and a man toiled up from the basement. He recognised Phoebe and nodded. 'That poor girl's place? Right, you go on up. I won't offer to come, my chest is bad today.' He was breathing noisily. Behind him came a rangy terrier dog who studied them with aggressive eyes. 'It's all right, he doesn't bite.'

'I wouldn't count on it,' said Phoebe as they climbed the stairs. 'He looked keen for a nip.'

'Or even a big bite. Did you see his teeth? Kept well sharpened.'

There was one door at the top of the stairs, where a card said: Miss Rice. Please ring the bell.

They did not have to ring the bell. The door was opened for them by a sturdy lady wearing denim trousers and a long apron.

'Thank you,' said Coffin.

'Knew you were on the way up. Fred rang from below to tell me. Security, you see, he looks after us.'

I don't know about Fred, thought Coffin, but I bet the dog could do a good job.

'He knew who you were, of course, he wouldn't just send anyone up.'

'And you?' Coffin was polite.

'You don't know me? I'm Mrs Rice, Mary's mother. I've come round here to tidy things up. You have to do that, don't you, when someone dies?' Her eyes filled with tears. 'Especially if they go so sharp and soon and unexpected as my poor girl did.'

'Yes,' said Coffin gently.

They all went to the small sitting room which already looked empty. Clearly, Mrs Rice was a fast worker. Several large black plastic sacks showed where she had stowed objects away. Books and clothes seemed to be most of what was there.

'Your lot came in and took away everything they wanted,' she said to Coffin.

'Of course,' Coffin was soothing this time.

'Gave me a list of what they took... nothing much really, not that Mary had much, bless her, and she'd only been in this place a few months. I wanted her to stay with me but no, she wanted her own place. Of course, I knew why she wanted it, I don't live such a sheltered life that I didn't realise she liked to have a boyfriend around sometimes. So, did we in my day, but we mostly did it in the old car or in the shed behind the gas works. Now they want a bed and breakfast after these days and good luck to them, I say, and why not?'

It was quite a speech.

While Coffin was listening, Phoebe had been walking round the room, trying to assess what she saw.

Not much, was the answer.

She couldn't get much of an impression of the sort of person that Mary had been but that might be because Mrs Rice's cleaning and effacing hand had already passed over the room.

Liked a bit of sex, according to her mum, but was not looking for a long term partner, enjoyed the company of her friends, and was keen on her work. Good at it, Phoebe judged, since she could not see how you could enjoy working on computers if you were not good at it. She had a small portable and a printer on a desk in the corner of the room.

No pictures of the boyfriends, so either Mary had not collected pictures of past lovers or the police teams had taken them away.

Mrs Rice did not seem to be the type to edit them away: a cleaner, yes, a censor, no. In fact, there had been a gleam in her eye that suggested otherwise.

'It's a bit bare, I know, but I've cleared out a lot of the clutter. Mary did like her odds and ends. I haven't thrown them away, of course. ' She looked at the plastic sack, 'but I've put them away. Till later.'

'I understand,' said Phoebe. 'Later, you might really want to look over the things that you've packed away.'

Mrs Rice nodded. 'Superintendent Miller understood too when he came.'

'Did he? When was that?'

'Day before last. Just a sympathy call.'

On the wall was a theatrical poster, large, old and yellowing. It advertised a pantomime. A tiny girl, dressed as a fairy, was shown dancing, dancing, dancing.

Lorry Love.

'That was her,' said Mrs Rice. 'Mary was Lorry Love.'

Another poster, more recent, was close to it.

'She looked a dear,' said Phoebe.

'Yes,' said Coffin. 'And she had talent too, I remember.'

'Her dancing career didn't last once she got bigger... too tall, you see. After about ten, no one wanted her. She minded a bit at first, but she got used to it. Did other things. Clever girl.'

'A shame,' said Coffin.

'She never got a big part, often in work though,' said

her mother, her voice proud, 'You know she was once in a pantomime as a child with Stella Pinero.'

Coffin hadn't known this, nor could he visualise his Stella as either Cinderella or the Fairy Godmother. She might have made a splendid Wicked Fairy, though.

They were granted a tour of the apartment which revealed something of the young woman who had lived there: she kept it tidy, she was her mother's daughter after all, she had some possessions but not many to judge by the few that her mother had assembled, her real life was lived elsewhere.

'No pictures of the men she knew.'

'I expect her mother cleared them away,' said Phoebe.

'No, I don't think so, she did it herself. Tidied each one away when his time was up.'

'Cold.'

'No, just someone who knew how to run her life.'

'While she had one,' Phoebe said, with some bitterness.

Mrs Rice appeared to ask if they would like a cup of tea. 'Got the kettle on the boil. You both look as though you could do with something. Not a very jolly business, what you've got to do.'

'No, it isn't,' agreed Coffin. 'Yes, thanks for the offer. We'd like it, wouldn't we, Phoebe?'

Surprised, Phoebe agreed they would.

'Not Mary's tea or sugar,' said Mrs Rice, 'just some of me own I brought round. Wouldn't use Mary's, wouldn't seem right somehow. Call me fanciful, but that's how I feel.'

'I know how you feel.'

She wasn't sure if she did, but it seemed the right thing to say.

'I wish I had some idea who killed the girls... I'd tell you if I did.'

'I know you would. If anything comes to you that might be helpful let me know.'

'She makes a good cup of tea,' said Phoebe, as they left. 'I didn't know what to make of her quite. I thinks she knows more about her daughter's life than she lets on, protecting her, I suppose.'

'Bit late for that. But you might ask her. Call again and see what you can get out of her,' suggested Coffin.

'OK, I will. If I can. She might be covering up for her daughter. It's what mothers do.'

'Some mothers,' said Coffin, thinking of his own mother and her disappearing act. 'Actually, go back in now and see if she will talk to you. I think I alarm her.'

'What? More than me?'

'I think so. I'll sit in the car and wait.'

Phoebe was longer than Coffin had expected. When she got back she quietly tucked herself in the driving seat and drove off without saying a word.

Then she said: 'She thinks her daughter may have known the serial killer.'

'Why? '

'Apparently Mary said something like 'Oh it's him,' when they were talking about the serial killer one day.'

'Is that all? she didn't give a name or a clue as to who she was talking about?'

'No.'

'You'd think her mother would have asked for a bit more detail.'

'She also thought he had help. She said that much.'

'Damn lot of use that is to us.'

'She didn't know her daughter was going to be killed. But we agree, don't we? About the helper?'

'Possibly,' said Coffin, who did not feel like agreeing with anything until he had spoken with all the forensic and scientific experts to see what they had to say. Not that he would necessarily agree with them either.

'Where's the next address?' he asked.

Phoebe fumbled with her papers; she did not usually fumble but her boss was making her nervous.

'In order of killing then that is Phillida Jessup although I don't know if it's the nearest address.'

'Let's go and have a cappuccino and think things over,' said Coffin.

Phoebe was surprised at this offer by her usually austere chief. 'Is there anywhere near where we can get one?'

'We can go to Mimsie Marker's. Her stall is not far away. ' He began to drive away. 'She's spreading too, she'll soon have an empire.'

Mimsie watched them approach. 'Not seen you two together recently,' she said, folding her arms on her ample waist. Fashionably dressed, though, Mimsie always dressed well.

'Work,' said Coffin. 'And now we need some coffee, good and strong but with some cream.'

'Treating yourself, eh?' asked Mimsie, starting the preparation.

'A case like this you need it.'

'Then I bet I know the case it is.' As she spoke she was pouring out the coffee and getting ready to carry it over to them.

A curving bench ran round one side of her stall with a shade over it to keep off sun and rain. Mimsie herself was well protected from the elements.

Coffin went up to get the coffee and to pay for it. The cappuccino looked good and strong, creamy on top and dark brown underneath. If anything could make Mimsie talk as you wished on the topic you wished (for talk she always would) it was praising her coffee.

'This is powerful coffee, Mimsie, just what I need today.'

'It's that serial killer,' she declared, 'Knew it was soon as I saw you both. Written in your faces. Rotten business.'

Coffin did not deny it.

'Take my advice, check the girls, find out what they had in common. You'll find the reason they were killed there. I know the theory is that these multiple killers strike at random... well some may, but I believe they go to each victim for a particular reason... find it and you are almost there.'

As Coffin began to make an acerbic response, a clutch of business men came up to get some lunch and a cup of coffee so the conversation had to stop.

Phoebe and Coffin enjoyed their coffee together with the piece of special shortcake that Mimsie had added.

'Now where is it that Jessup lived?'

Thought you never forgot anything, said Phoebe to herself, as she consulted her list. 'Six, Murt Terrace.'

'And where is that?'

'Thought you'd know, it's the road behind the old hall that the theatre uses for one of its rehearsal rooms. Lady Coffin would know it.' And I bet you do, she said to herself, but for some reason you don't want to say so.

'Murt Terrace? We'd better go there then.'

'Know the way, sir?'

'I can find it.' As of course, he could, it was the place where he and Stella had once parted forever.

Well, for twenty-four hours. And it had been Stella who had given way and rushed to come back to him.

But the pain while he wondered if he would see her again had been real enough, It came back sharply as they drove down Murt Terrace, a row of neat little houses like much of this part of the Second City.

Mrs Jessup, for she had been married once, lived on her own with no sister or mother to check on her empty home. Someone would in the end, but they had not done so far. It looked neglected.

'We can get in,' said Phoebe. 'I came here originally myself.'

'I didn't know she was one of yours.'

'She wasn't. I came with Les.'

'Let us in then, Phoebe.'

Phillida Jessup had lived in the whole little house which she had kept neat and tidy. Now it just felt empty, the owner was dead and the house knew it.

Coffin and Phoebe stood on the threshold. 'She hasn't left much around,' complained Phoebe. 'I thought that when I came with Les. He was quite put out, he likes things to sort over.'

'Let's go in,' said Coffin, leading the way.

There was an entrance hall, narrow and neatly carpeted with a sitting room on one side, the kitchen next to it and the bedroom and bedroom facing each other across the corridor upstairs. The classic two up, two down, now back in fashion.

'That's it,' said Phoebe. 'Of course, the forensic boys have been in but even they haven't made much of a mess for once.'

'Look in the wastepaper bins again,' said the knowledgeable Coffin. 'I know you looked once but things get passed over sometimes as you just discovered at Amy Buckly's. And the odds and ends can tell you a lot about a person's character.'

Phoebe frowned at him. 'I knew what I was doing,' she allowed herself.

'Of course you did,' said Coffin soothingly. 'But it's worth a look.' He was taking one himself. 'Only torn up paper here,' he said of the basket in the kitchen. He was examining them, confident that Phoebe had done so already. Just small bills, mostly for food.

He went on into the bedroom. The basket by the bed table was a pretty blue to match the wallpaper.

Phoebe watched him from the door. 'Only a bundle of used theatre tickets in there.'

'So I see, a play my *wife* was in.' He looked at Phoebe without speaking.'

'She has a lot of fans,' Phoebe said.

They went on to the bathroom, finding nothing there. It was tidy, bare, with the towels neatly arranged.

'Do you think she knew she wouldn't be back?' said Coffin.

'No,' said Phoebe vehemently. 'Do we go on?'

'Yes.' Coffin was clear. 'Angela Dover next, then the body in Pepper Alley... Lotty Brister, wasn't it?'

Angela Dover had her own house in Greenwich not far from where she worked. She shared it with another woman, Hester Carter. Miss Carter did not seem pleased to see them.

'You lot back again? What is it this time? You couldn't stop Angie getting killed.'

'We can find out who did though,' said Coffin.

'Oh, do you think so? Then you must be cleverer than you look.'

Coffin thought about it for a minute. 'We are,' he said. 'Can we walk round the rooms that Angela used?'

'If you must. Get on with it. Five minutes.'

Coffin went into Angela's sitting room and then her bedroom. Phoebe, rightly interpreting Coffin's look, stayed behind to keep Hester Carter in talk.

Coffin went round the bedroom and sitting room, they were tidy, as if Hester had already been in there. A pile of theatre programmes on a desk interested him. They were all recent, so perforce featured his wife.

Where did Stella come in all this?

He thanked Hester as he emerged. She gave him a small nod, not unfriendly but not especially warm either.

'You'll miss her,' he said.

'We didn't live in each other's pockets, but yes, of course I will.'

'It's good to have company for the theatre or any outing,' said Coffin.

Hester did not answer but politely showed him to the door. 'Seen all you want? I hope you catch him.'

'Didn't like her much,' said Phoebe as they left.

'She was more polite towards the end. I think she was very fond of Angela.'

'Did you get anything useful?'

Coffin didn't answer and Phoebe knew from experience you did not push him.

Finally there was the home of Lotty Brister to go to. Lotty was so far the last body. She was the oldest of all the victims.

She had been cast aside in her working clothes her body was dropped in the gutter.

The two stood outside her house. Not a smart address, but there were window boxes full of geraniums, red and white, while a tabby cat sat on the doorstep.

'I don't think I need to go in,' said Coffin. 'Lotty is one on her own, she isn't part of the series. I feel sure of that. She doesn't match.' As they turned back to their car, he said he hoped someone was looking after the cat, but even as he spoke the front door was opened and the cat went in. Vaguely cheered, Coffin started the car. Someone was living there.

'Three more dead,' he said thoughtfully, 'We haven't talked about the bodies just found, or poor Charlie Fisher.' He added: 'The three found at the theatre were the first to die, you know. I had the pathologist's report this morning. I'd been told verbally, of course.'

'You think these earlier deaths are connected with the serial killings?'

'They are all part of the crime pattern somehow. The lad's death could be suicide, after killing the girl and the child - he had failed to get the prize of best young actor. Everyone agrees he was depressed. So he killed the girl and their child.'

'And then killed himself?'

'He was preparing to, I think, but someone else may have done it for him. Then buried him. And just where Stella was preparing to build... I don't like it.'

Phoebe was silent. Coffin was not a man to let his imagination run away with him, although the said imagination was a powerful machine inside him which had helped him as a detective. She was more limited herself and she knew it.

'And today. You noticed I'm sure, although you didn't say anything, that somehow Stella and the theatre crept into the background of every girl except the last, and there might have been something there if we'd really looked... It's like a terrible ballet with all dancing to the same music and all in pain.'

'Now that really is over the top,' said Phoebe.

To her relief, Coffin grinned at her. 'Yes, you're right. I must be more rational.'

He drove Phoebe back to the Headquarters. On the way they passed the big teaching hospital. He saw a familiar figure swing past him towards the entrance.

'There's Joe Jones. Going to the hospital. I hope he's not ill.'

Then he remembered: his wife worked there.

Another car followed Joe's in.

'That's Mercy Adams,' said Phoebe. 'Are they together?'

Chapter 17

Mercy Adams parked her car near to Joe's. Far from being with Joe, she had not even been aware he was there in the hospital. She was going to visit her boyfriend, Dr Stephen Wrong.

She was going to tell Stephen that she was not pregnant and never had been. She did not know if he would be pleased or not. He had sounded excited at the idea of a child.

'Marriage, why not? And you can give up this terrible work you do.'

He did not like the idea of Mercy as a detective, especially when the crime was murder.

'But you are very interested in it, you question me about it, and you must read all the details in the newspapers because you always know the details before I tell you,' she said. 'Sometimes, I think you know more than I do.' She had no intention of giving up her work, especially as he seemed to find it so absorbing too.

He hadn't cared for that, had denied it indignantly moving them into one of their very rare quarrels.

'But if we don't fight,' Mercy said to herself, 'it's because I watch my tongue.'

Mercy was worried about Dr Wrong. To her mind he took too keen an interest in the serial murders.

He was a doctor, so perhaps his desire for detail was understandable, but she thought his interest obsessive. She knew, although he had not told her, that he had got into the morgue to see at least two of the bodies when they were being investigated.

An outsider, someone who did know him as well as she did, might be suspicious of him.

Doctors could be killers, Phoebe had suggested as much the other day.

Had he really said "they cut up beautifully"?

'You could be a killer yourself,' she'd said, a case of not watching her tongue, at which he had been very angry. Anyway he was not a surgeon but on the medical side, working with allergies.

She felt split loyalties; she was going to see Dr Wrong to say that it might be better if they didn't see each other again.

At least not while the murder investigation went on.

Mercy had hinted to Phoebe about her worries over Stephen and considered talking to Les Henderson or Winnie Ardet but so far she had said nothing officially. It didn't seem fair to Stephen somehow. So she had been keeping quiet.

She was careful about talking to John Coffin. He was the big boss, you only went to him when you had a very good reason, as she had done before. He had a reputation for being both kind and perceptive, but he was also formidable. Stella Pinero, his actress wife, was more easily approached but she was intensely loyal to her husband.

Stephen Wrong was sitting at his desk studying some records. He looked up, pleased to see Mercy.

He stood up and came up to her. 'Nice to see you.' He studied her face. 'That's good, it's a smile. You've been giving me some strange looks lately, That's the worst of being a copper, I suppose, you worry about everyone. Come and have some coffee and talk. I'm fond of you, Mercy, perhaps more than that. We could be happy together but not if you are going to keep looking at me as if I am raping the cat.'

'You *have* worried me,' said Mercy. The hospital canteen was quiet for once, and the coffee hot and good. 'I suppose I have been over-imaginative.'

'About me you have. You ought to look closer home.'

As she drank, he went into details.

'I see what you mean,' said Mercy.

'I hope you do. I wondered whether to speak to you or not because you are part of the team investigating the killer. That's why I have been so curious.'

Mercy nodded. Then she frowned. 'Oh, I don't know, it is just so hard for me to suspect that particular person.'

The Chief Commander had seen both Mercy and Joe go into the hospital.

'Working?' he asked Phoebe. 'Are they both working?'

'Could be. It may be nothing.'

'It's when you think it may be nothing that it's worth taking a look.' In fact, he had a very clear suspicion inside him. He was not passing just by chance, after all. His suspicions had been growing for some time now, but without any hard evidence. Perhaps now was the chance he had needed.

He drove to the police HQ where he dropped Phoebe, then told her he planned to go to the hospital. She offered to come with him, but Coffin refused.

'I'll just go on my own and take a look round. Casual. It'll seem more official if you come with me.'

'I'd better come,' Phoebe insisted.

'No, if I'm not in touch in half an hour, you can come then. Bring Les Henderson if he is around.'

Before going he telephoned Stella. She came out of a rehearsal to speak to him. 'What is it?' She wasn't too pleased to be interrupted.

'I'm off to the University Hospital. No, nothing wrong with me, but I think something is going on there and I want to find out what.'

Then he told her what he wanted her to do in certain circumstances.

Coffin drove back quickly to the hospital. There were three entrances so he chose the one which Inspector Jones had used. Joe might need help.

He walked in to a long and busy corridor with sub corridors opening off it. No sign of Mercy or Joe.

He walked slowly down towards the end where large

doors opened on to a big ward. He didn't expect to see Mercy or Joe in there.

'What am I doing?' he asked himself. 'Wasting my time.' But he kept on walking. Then out of the crowds passing all around him, a nurse came up to him.

'Chief Commander Coffin?'

He stopped. 'Yes?'

She was a pretty young woman, but her face looked tired. 'I'm Charge Nurse Pritchard.' She looked too young to have a lot of responsibility but she also looked efficient. 'I went to a talk you gave once so I recognised you.'

He looked at her. One of the Coffin fan club? No, she was in earnest about a real problem.

'I was looking for someone to report to and all our security men seem absent...' She gave Coffin a charming smile. 'So I was glad to see you.'

'How can I help?'

'I think there's something going on in the side office on Ward E. It's a waiting room for general use.'

'What sort of something?'

'Maybe a fight,' she said. 'It sounded serious.'

'Take me there.' Coffin ordered.

She led him through the crowd, then took a side turn down a short corridor. A big door led to Ward E, but at the end of the passage there on the left there was another door.

The nurse nodded towards it. 'In there.'

Coffin could see through the glass door. There were four people in there: two women and two men. He knew them all but felt surprise all the same. This was not what he had expected to find.

'I know the doctor and the nurse but do you know the other man?'

Coffin took a long, thoughtful look. 'Oh yes. I know him. '

He said in a low voice. 'One of my officers... Inspector Joe Jones.' He felt more shocked than he could show.

Joe was holding a knife, with a gun in his other hand.

'You'd better get away.'

'What about you?'

'I'll be all right,' said Coffin. 'I doubt if he will attack me although he may want to.'

Privately he was not so sure.

'He won't touch me.' In fact he was far from sure - perhaps Joe wanted him as well as Stella. Or was it Joe's wife, that tall, lean angry figure by his side?

'I've never been quite sure if you are man or woman,' Coffin thought to himself. 'And I don't believe you know either.'

He pushed open the door. 'Well, Joe, so this is it?'

Nurse Pritchard called after him: 'I'll get help.'

Coffin strode into the room. 'I didn't know the killer was you, Joe.'

'Who said it was?'

'I do. But why?' The obvious question, but somehow he had to ask it.

A voice from the other side of the room spoke up: 'The dead boy, the one dug up, was my son... Joe's stepson... he wanted to win the prize and position as actor that your wife Stella was offering... he didn't get it, so he killed himself and his woman and his child. We buried him where it would do most damage to Stella Pinero.'

Coffin looked towards the tall, thin, figure of Joe's wife. She was wearing a trouser suit and managed to look more masculine than Joe. She continued in a harsh voice.

'I had to avenge him. So I killed the Stella Freaks...'

'Yes, I had noticed the connection.'

'I'd have had *her* in the end.'

Coffin was silent, but he gritted his teeth.

'Don't blame Joe... he's a little bit mad as you may have noticed. And I enjoyed the killings. You can, you know. Or do you?' She looked questioningly at Coffin.

'Over the years, I have learnt that sad truth,' said Coffin.

Josephine went over to stand beside her husband. He had his gun and knife, she too carried a knife.

The bond between them would have been touching if it hadn't been so terrible. Can you catch madness? Coffin asked himself.

'Some of you may get out of here alive, but I'm not sure who.' Josephine faced them defiantly.

Mercy leaned against the wall, she looked as though she was on the point of fainting. Dr Stephen Wrong had his arms round her.

Coffin took a breath. 'You must think I am a fool... Do you really think I came here tonight without back up?' He had to keep talking because Mercy was pulling herself together and edging towards Joe and his wife.

'Phoebe and Stella and I have a code. When I told them tonight I was coming here, they knew to send some support.'

Of course he had his mobile telephone in a convenient pocket, but sometimes the sight of the telephone in use provoked danger. So he said a silent prayer that Stella would get it right.

Stella did know what she had to do and it involved sending a message to tell Paul Masters to send help. Les Henderson and Phoebe too. She had her instructions.

Stella had been told: 'If I don't telephone you once within the first half hour then tell Paul Masters to see I get help. Ask Les to come with the unit. Phoebe will know where, Paul Masters can empower everything. But Les is the one to come. He may have to look for me, but he's clever.'

'Do I come too?' Stella had asked, and got a firm NO. ' I don't want you mixed up in it.'

'But I *am* mixed up in it,' she had protested: 'I didn't know all the women, but I bet they all knew me.'

Stella Pinero, famous actress and the power behind the theatre complex she had created for the Second City, was a vital part of this series of murders. She was the cause, she knew it. She didn't know why, but it all revolved around her and the theatre.

What she didn't say to him was that she felt their ghosts pressing down on her head with every day that passed.

So she watched and when she saw Les setting out, with two supporters, not police constables she knew but she recognised their style - toughies - she followed. Les soon saw that she was following him and he knew that the Chief Commander would not want her there because of the very real danger she would be in. But she was the Guvnor's wife and he did not feel able to stop her.

There was Phoebe following him, as well, he saw.

Between the two of them, they might manage to lose Stella inside the hospital. But she was out of her car, parked and going through the hospital with her eyes fixed on him. She was just behind him.

He swung round to face her. 'Miss Pinero, Lady Coffin.'

'Make up your mind.' She kept her tone gentle but he could feel the whip of anger.

'Do not follow me. '

'Did he tell you to stop me?' She held out her hand to grab Phoebe who had drawn level with them.

'No, but I know he told you to stay away.'

'How do you know?'

'I'm a detective, Miss Pinero.'

'I am sure that he has got hold of the serial killer and that I am part of the motive. I want to be there.'

She could not get past him without pushing.

'Lady Pinero, Lady Coffin...' he was flustered, but he got himself together. 'Stella, the man in there... he abducted you once.'

'I got away.'

'He let you go... he wanted to prolong the game, that's what the Chief Commander thinks,' Les was talking fast, anxious to get where he was needed. 'If you follow me, you will be playing his game, and he will kill you. In front of your husband. Stay with Phoebe.' Phoebe nodded as if she understood. She probably did. He wished to hell he did.

Stella stared at him without speaking.

'There is no death penalty now, remember,' said Les. 'You will be dead and he will be alive, you will have given him victory.'

From a double door on their left there came the sound of raised voices.

Stella knew the voice of her husband while Les Henderson knew the grindingly angry voice that was answering him.

If it was an answer, it sounded more like an attack.

Ignoring Stella, he nodded to his two companions, specially chosen officers, and pushed open the door.

All the same, it could have been a bit quicker, Coffin thought - why the hell had Les and Co. been such a while coming. He must remember to find out, he decided as he pressed the wound on his arm where the blood was dripping, and kept his other arm tightly round Joe's neck while Mercy gripped the woman, arms behind her.

At least it had given him time to ask what he had needed to know.

'Why the hell did you involve the lad Charlie, cut his fingers off?'

'To keep him from sticking his fingers into my life. He was a nosey little bugger.'

No answer really Coffin thought. Joe was mad so he kept his own fingers tight round his neck.

Although it could have been a speedier rescue, it had been a comfort to see Les and his cohorts rush in.

When it came down to it, neither Joe nor his wife struggled that much. Perhaps they had wanted to be caught, you never knew.

Later that evening Stella gave a her husband a loving look. 'You were lucky to get away with a slashed arm.'

Then she asked the question on her mind: 'What will happen to Joe and his wife?

'A more comfortable fate than that of their victims,' replied Coffin. 'The wife might get off if she has a good lawyer although to my mind she was as much if not more guilty than her husband. No, she won't get off, forget I said that, she was the one who stole the uterus and made use of it, although why or what good it did we may never know. Might find out if she talks. But he will go down as her mad mentor, I expect. As a former police man he won't have an altogether easy time. To rape and kill all those women with her encouragement he doesn't deserve it anyway.'

'Good,' said Stella with some satisfaction.

They were back in the comfortable sitting room of their home in the tower. They knew now why the three bodies, so close to where they lived and underneath what would have been Stella's latest workplace, had been buried there.

To haunt Stella.

They were already doing so.

Gus the dog sat at Coffin's feet. He could smell blood, and having undergone a serious operation himself he was prepared to be sympathetic.

The cat also smelt blood which was of interest, there might be something to hunt or to eat. Coffin, fortunately, did not know he was being assessed as eatable, so he reached out to pat the cat's head.

'If you have to get knifed, I suppose a hospital is as good a place as any,' said Coffin. He added indignantly: 'Do you know, they wanted to keep me in. I wouldn't allow it.'

Stella said:' It's ruined that tweed jacket... Still, I never liked it, it wasn't worthy of you.' She tidied the jacket away. 'What about the paedophile cases? You haven't mentioned them.'

'Not much progress there, but we'll get there.'

Stella thought she had heard that before. She smiled and shook her head.

'End of story, my love.'

Except that, as Coffin knew all too well, there were always questions at the end of each case. Probably it had been Joe who had planted the mannequin. But Coffin knew it was Josephine who had dressed it to look like Stella. She had boasted of it. The store of props had been uncovered.

Something would have to be done, also, about the letters Joe Jones had sent to confuse the paedophile investigation. It had set them back considerably. He must have been ill for longer than anyone realised. Corruption had run deep in him.

No case ever really ended with a full stop, he thought. You always went on wondering.